To Betsy,
Happy Reading!
Carrie
xxx

Carrie Hope Fletcher is an actress, singer and vlogger. Carrie has starred in a number of shows in London's West End and on national theatre tours, including *Les Misérables*, *The Addams Family*, *Heathers*, *Andrew Lloyd Webber's Cinderella* and more. She has written several bestselling books for adults and children.

Carrie lives just outside of London with her husband, Joel, Edgar the tuxedo cat and many fictional friends that she keeps on her bookshelves – just in case she wants an adventure.

CARRIE HOPE FLETCHER

Illustrated by Davide Ortu

PUFFIN

PUFFIN BOOKS

UK | USA | Canada | Ireland | Australia
India | New Zealand | South Africa

Puffin Books is part of the Penguin Random House group of companies
whose addresses can be found at global.penguinrandomhouse.com

www.penguin.co.uk
www.puffin.co.uk
www.ladybird.co.uk

First published 2023
001

Set in 13.3/18 pt Bembo Book MT Pro
Typeset by Jouve (UK), Milton Keynes
Printed and bound in Great Britain by Clays Ltd, Elcograf S.p.A.

The authorized representative in the EEA is Penguin Random House Ireland,
Morrison Chambers, 32 Nassau Street, Dublin D02 YH68

A CIP catalogue record for this book is available from the British Library

HARDBACK
ISBN: 978–0–241–55894–2

INTERNATIONAL PAPERBACK
ISBN: 978–0–241–55895–9

All correspondence to:
Puffin Books
Penguin Random House Children's
One Embassy Gardens, 8 Viaduct Gardens, London SW11 7BW

To every child who reads this book. You have so much magic within you. Use it to light your way through darkness.

Contents

Prologue

The first day of school is always frightening. Moving up a year involves new teachers and textbooks, new facts and fractions, new words and bigger ones at that! But, for an entirely new student, a first day also brings the unpleasant possibility of not fitting in right away and potentially eating lunch alone, wondering if every new face is friend or foe.

If a new student happened to be particularly prone to worrying, they might not sleep the night before and instead spend the entire time staring wide-eyed at the ceiling, fearing the worst, terrified that not only will they not know any of the answers in class, but everyone, teachers and students alike, will hate their guts.

That's what it was like for Harriet Harper, anyway. She'd just moved to Crowood Peak, and the thought of not making any friends was her worst fear. Harriet hadn't had many friends before. She thought maybe it was because she was a little bit odd. She wasn't allowed friends round for tea, she'd never had a birthday party or a sleepover, and if she was ever invited to other children's houses, she had to turn down the invitation right away. She loved her family, but she recognized that they were . . . different.

At her old school, most children were dropped off at the gates in ordinary cars with school bags packed neatly and their ordinary lunch boxes filled with ordinary cheese-and-pickle sandwiches. Harriet's grandma, on the other hand, insisted on driving Harriet to school in the sidecar of her motorbike that left a trail of smoke wherever it went. Harriet's school bag always had the right textbooks, but there were usually pages missing or they were chewed at the edges. Her teacher never believed her excuse that the dog ate her homework, mainly because she didn't have a dog. And at lunchtime no one ever sat next to her due to the fact that her lunch often consisted of a huge slab of meat (usually very rare). Her dad had been a butcher then, you see, and was very serious about the subject.

'It's all about the protein!' he'd say at dinner as he carved yet another thick joint of beef.

Harriet's family and their odd ways certainly lost her the few friends she had at her old school. After a while, everyone stopped inviting her, and a while after that they stopped hanging out with her altogether. Harriet knew there was a good reason she wasn't allowed to do all the things other kids could do, so she didn't dare complain too much. She just wished things were different.

So Harriet Harper decided to put her best foot forward on her first day at school in Crowood Peak and dressed herself in her favourite outfit. She donned her leather jacket, which was covered in thorns from all her favourite roses (she'd sewn them on herself). She painted her lips the darkest shade of black she had (it was called Bottomless Pit), and she styled her raven-black hair the best way she knew how: with an entire can of hairspray misted from root to tip so almost every strand zigzagged away from her face like lightning bolts. She'd also painted her nails a bright blood-red to finish off the whole look.

Harriet dressed this way to outwardly reflect how she wanted to be. Someone cool and confident. Someone who didn't jump at shadows or feel tears prickle the backs of their eyes when they felt the least bit anxious or scared. She dressed like the person she longed to be in an attempt to hide the person she was.

Harriet stared into the mirror and smiled. She was nervous, sure, but this was a fresh new start.

On the other side of town, Orville Thomas was also a little nervous on his first day at school, but it was mixed with a huge slice of thrill. Yes, Orville had been *thrilled* to move to Crowood Peak. It was a small town, but it had so much history.

He wasn't worried about making friends because he seemed to find that quite easy, no matter where he went. Maybe that's because he had no real interest in making friends, so the ones he did make were simply a bonus. School was about learning, but Orville also had a secret mission, and he intended to keep his eyes on the prize.

He packed his brown satchel with a notepad and a pencil case filled until it was bursting at the seams with pens in all different colours. He slid his arms into the tweed jacket passed down to him by his dad, who'd got it from his dad, who'd got it from his dad, who'd got it from his dad, who'd got it from his, and from his, and from his, and from his, who'd got it from his brother! It was still in perfect condition and had all the names of those who had worn it before Orville embroidered on the back. Every one of them had sewn their name themself, and Orville intended to do so as well (which meant he'd have to learn how first, but he'd cross that bridge when he came to it).

The final thing Orville needed before heading to his new school was his camera, which was on a black leather strap around his neck, ready to snap his first pictures of Crowood Peak.

Spencer Sparrow also loved taking photos, but mainly of himself. He snapped a selfie on his phone, then looked at it and sighed. Spencer took great pride in his appearance. He always styled his red hair in a quiff with one curl that coiled down the centre of his forehead. He wore his favourite earrings, which looked like little spiders and hung down from his ears as if they were dangling from a web. Over his all-black outfit, he put on a floor-length velvet coat in his favourite colour, forest green (he'd painted his nails the night before to match).

Spencer threw his brown leather satchel over his shoulder, checked the weather to see that there was a thick cover of cloud over Crowood Peak that day and then didn't stop to say goodbye to his parents before sauntering out of the house with his trusty black umbrella tucked under his arm.

The early September mornings had a chill to them in Crowood Peak. All the leaves had begun to fall and settle like a crumpled orange blanket across the dewy grass. Harriet jumped in every puddle on her way to school and often stopped when the scent of someone's breakfast caught in her nostrils and made her belly growl.

Orville saw most of his journey to school through the lens of his camera and snapped at least fifty photographs before he got there. That was almost as many photographs as the number of times Spencer checked his quiff in any reflective surface he could find: car mirrors, shop windows, duck ponds, you name it. Yet he was still smoothing his hair when he arrived.

Amid the hustle and bustle on the path leading to the school, these three new students found themselves standing close together, gazing up at the gates. A mixture of terror and glee washed over them in the autumn breeze. Harriet, Orville and Spencer all drew a deep breath and took their first steps into Crowood School.

1
Magic in Crowood

Ever since Maggie and Ivy had helped banish the curse of the Crowood Witch, the Double Trouble Society had become (almost) *famous*. Everyone had wanted to shake hands with the witches and congratulate all the children on their triumph, but Maggie and Ivy became town heroes for a brief time. The mayor of Crowood Peak was quite beside himself trying to think of what he could do to commemorate their achievements.

'We could rename the library! How about the Eerie Tomb Library? Oh . . . no . . . that won't do at all! Perhaps something at the cemetery?'

'Honestly, Mr Mayor,' Ivy said, 'there's nothing we want. We're just happy everyone's safe and that Emerald's not evil any more.'

'Yeah,' added Maggie. 'You don't need to name anything after us. But maybe the occasional free biscuit or two from the Cosy Cauldron cafe wouldn't go amiss – OW!' She yelped as Ivy elbowed her.

'We don't want anything at all,' said Ivy firmly. 'We're just happy that everyone's safe.'

Maggie and Ivy were also happy because the Double Trouble Society now had LOADS of new members.

There was Maggie and Ivy, of course, but since the return of the Crowood Witch they'd recruited Eddie, the brightest boy in their year, and Isaac, who had the most curious and adventurous mind they knew. Then there was creative and crafty Jennifer, who had made them all their own broomsticks (whether they could fly them or not). Jamie had a real eye for fashion and made sure that everyone had the perfect costume for the upcoming Halloween bash. Jemima no longer had a bad thing to say about anyone (well, hardly ever . . .) and Darla was keen to learn what everyone had to teach her, like a little sponge soaking up all their knowledge.

Then, of course, there were the original members of the Double Trouble Society: Bill Eerie, Ivy's father, and Max Tomb, Maggie's dad. Bill and Max had been friends since they were at school together, and their antics had earned them the name the Double Trouble Society, given to them by their exasperated teachers. The two fathers then bestowed the name on their daughters when they appeared to be as inseparable as Bill and Max had been at that age.

After the shenanigans at last year's Festival for the Twelve, Bill and Max were thrilled to see the society they'd begun welcome so many new members. However, they did wish their first adventure had been a little less . . . rocky. (Occasionally, both Bill and Max still found tiny bits of gravel stuck in their teeth after being turned to stone by the Crowood Witch, but they were mostly just happy to be alive.)

Finally, the newest and arguably most exciting recruits to the Double Trouble Society were the twin-sister witches, Amethyst and Emerald. They had joined after all the very scary goings-on during the last blue moon and Emerald's regrettable attempt to eat the heart of a Crowood child. She didn't, though, and swore hand on heart that she wouldn't ever attempt to do so again.

After something like that, however, it did prove a little hard to gain everyone's trust. Luckily, when Amethyst and Emerald proved what an asset two magical beings could be to the little town of Crowood, everyone fell in love with them.

Amethyst's and Emerald's powers were very different and served two very different purposes. Amethyst was a moon witch, meaning that she was most powerful at night-time. If anyone had trouble sleeping, Amethyst could not only help them doze off quickly and peacefully, but she could give them happier dreams too. If any nocturnal creatures were rooting through bins or digging up flower beds, Amethyst was able to talk to them and politely ask them to stop.

She was also incredible at making potions using moon water. This was any rainwater that Amethyst had collected under a full moon and 'charged'. She used it in almost all her spells like a cook would add salt and pepper.

Emerald, on the other hand, drew her power from the earth. Since she'd arrived, it was as if the ground beneath her feet had sensed her presence and come alive. Suddenly the grass was greener, and trees sprang to life and bore fruit when before you'd be lucky to get a single apple. Flowers bloomed wherever she walked, and she had helped everyone's gardens grow and become prettier than ever before.

However, now that autumn was here, it was the most colourful season the people of Crowood Peak had ever seen. The chestnuts were so big you could barely hold one in your palm; there were so many apples and blackberries that Mrs Anderson, the owner of the Cosy Cauldron, couldn't bake pies fast enough.

Emerald had even managed to grow things that never grew, and would never grow, in Crowood like cinnamon, bananas and pineapples. There was no limit to what she could make sprout from the earth, and this meant that everyone's kitchens and tummies were full, and everyone's gardens and vases were even fuller. Crowood Peak was a happier and more spectacular place because of the two witches.

Amethyst and Emerald also couldn't believe their luck. While not everyone had been accepting of them (some people still crossed the street when passing Hokum House and others steered their children away from the two witches in the supermarket), most of the townsfolk had embraced them, powers and all. It meant more to Amethyst and Emerald than they were able to explain, so they showed their gratitude through their magic.

For every apple crumble and rhubarb pie they were given, Amethyst made sure Mrs Anderson had the most beautiful dreams. For every glowing story Max wrote about them in the local newspaper, Amethyst gave him a potion to improve his cooking (although this was mostly because she was fed up of the smell of smoke pouring from his kitchen window every morning when he burned toast or bacon or, on one occasion, the orange juice!). Every time Max and Bill allowed Maggie and Ivy to come to Hokum House for dinner, the two witches made sure the girls went home with tummies full of the most delicious food and heads filled with only happy thoughts.

They had also started their own cleaning business in Crowood Peak. For those who were happy to accept magic into their homes, Amethyst and Emerald had come up with a range of magical products that eliminated the need to do chores. No matter how dirty the self-cleaning dishes got, once you'd finished your meal, you just had to put them in a cupboard, close the door and say, 'Save me a job and clean yourselves!' The next time you looked, they'd be so clean and sparkly you could use them as a mirror!

The soak-and-sweep was a very well-mannered mop-and-broom set that got to work when you left the house. They worked as a team to make sure the floors were spotless by the time you came home.

Then there was the spray that made your house smell like your favourite things – freshly mown grass or gingerbread warm from the oven! All you had to do was think about the scent you wanted and then squirt the bottle. Some people made their homes smell like orange groves, some went for campfires on the beach and others chose freshly folded linen.

All in all, Crowood Peak had become a wonderful place to live, and there was no more talk of demons or curses or eating hearts. Just magic and dreams and hope for the future of the town and its children.

THE END

Ha! Did you really think that was it? No chance! There's much more to come – all kinds of spooks and scares – just you wait. Keep reading to find out what scrape the Double Trouble Society have got themselves into this time.

2
Darkness Returns

'Do I even *want* to know what's in this?' Maggie asked. She was perched on the top of a little stepladder, holding up a small jar to the kitchen light. It glowed a strange reddish brown colour and seemed to have little lumps that swished back and forth as the liquid sloshed about inside.

'Oh, that? That's just . . . actually, no. You don't want to know.' Amethyst laughed. 'I can tell you that it's very good for curing acute boredom, so if you're ever stuck for something to do on a rainy afternoon, just let me know and I'll give you a spoonful!'

Maggie removed the lid and gave the jar a sniff. It smelled like mackerel that had been left in the sun for a month. She gagged and quickly replaced the lid and tightened it as much as she could.

'Remind me never to be bored again!' She set the jar down on the table and pushed it as far away as possible.

Amethyst chuckled. 'See! It's already working!'

'What's it really for?' Ivy whispered when Maggie went back to removing jars from the back of the highest shelf in one of the Hokum House kitchen cupboards.

'Getting rid of warts!' Amethyst replied, and Ivy stifled a laugh with the sleeve of her pink cardigan.

They were giving the kitchen a thorough clear-out. Since Emerald and Amethyst had permanently moved to Crowood Peak, they'd been incredibly busy. Amethyst had never made so many potions, and Emerald had never grown so many flowers. This meant that their kitchen, the place Amethyst made her potions and the place Emerald cleaned up after a hard day in the garden, had become a place of complete chaos. There were empty jars everywhere, and the ones that were full contained liquids that looked even more questionable now than when they'd been fresh.

'Why do all the things that go into your potions look like they've come from a nearby pond?' asked Maggie, inspecting another jar.

'Well, it's probably because that one *did* come from a nearby pond. It's frogspawn. And it isn't for potions – I put it on my toast.' Maggie's mouth fell open.

'Oh, Maggie, you're so easy to wind up!'

Amethyst took the jar from her and carried it over to the large pewter cauldron in the fireplace. She dumped the contents into the pot, and the mixture made a noise like the one Emerald did after her first sip of a good cup of tea: *Aaahhhh!*

However, that was not what came out of Emerald's mouth as she burst through the back door of Hokum House at that very moment.

'EVIL!'

Emerald clutched the door frame to hold herself up. All the strength had left her body, and her face had gone grey, as if not just the colour had been sucked out of her but all the joy and happiness too.

Amethyst knew at once that all was no longer well in Crowood Peak. She immediately stopped what she was doing, dropping her large, long-handled silver spoon into the bubbling purple liquid she'd been stirring in the cauldron. It made a satisfying *SPLOSH* before sinking to the bottom.

'Sister? What is it? What's wrong?' Amethyst took Emerald's hands and led her over to a chair at the kitchen table. Maggie hopped down off her stepladder, and Ivy put down the potion book she'd been reading before rushing to

Emerald's side. Amethyst rubbed Emerald's fingers, which were ice-cold. It was chilly outside in the autumn air where Emerald had been tending the garden, but this was different. She felt deathly cold.

'Can't you *smell* it?' Emerald hissed, sniffing the air. She had spent three hundred years as a cat before transforming into the Crowood Witch, and her acute sense of smell had never left her.

Amethyst ran to the back door, stuck her head outside and took a deep breath, as hard and as long as she could. So hard her nostrils squeaked. There was something there, but she couldn't work out what it was, so she closed her eyes. Being a moon witch, her senses were always tuned into things that carried the same sort of magic, like the tides and the owls, and the thoughts of people who were very close to drifting off to sleep. Her magic was also at its strongest when the moon was full, so when it was waxing and waning it wasn't as powerful as Emerald's.

Amethyst concentrated with all her might, and then suddenly there it was. A sharp tang of brimstone hit her tongue and spread through her mouth. She gagged and almost vomited on the grass. It was like biting into a rotten egg.

Maggie and Ivy looked at each other questioningly. 'I can't smell anything,' said Maggie.

'He's here. He's coming for me.' Emerald was staring at the

kitchen table, her hands flat in front of her, fingers splayed and nails digging into the wood, leaving deep grooves. She began to move her fingers back and forth, scratching like a cat that was sharpening its claws ready to attack.

Amethyst wiped her mouth on the back of her sleevc, the skin underneath prickling with goose pimples. But she had a duty as a sister, as a twin. When one fell apart, the other needed to be strong.

'It was only a little hint of brimstone,' she said, almost gagging again. Emerald gave her a stern look.

'Even a hint could mean trouble, Amethyst. You know how quickly darkness can spread!'

'Well, it could be far worse.' Amethyst tried to smile. 'It took me a while to detect it, which means it really could be anything.' She laughed, a little hysterically and squawky. 'It could just be a . . . a . . . different demon. One that has nothing to do with the curse of the Crowood Witch. Let's not get ahead of ourselves and begin to panic unnecessarily before we really know what's going on, OK?'

'Hang on a second . . .' Ivy said. 'Are you talking about the demon that cursed the Crowood Witch three hundred years ago?'

'Surely he couldn't still be alive! He'd be *ancient*!' Maggie laughed, but she stopped abruptly when Amethyst and Emerald both pursed their lips into a thin, tight line. 'Wh–what? What did I say?'

'Maggie,' Ivy said, rolling her eyes, 'you do realize Emerald spent three hundred years as a cat, right? And Amethyst lived through all that time as well?'

'Technically, in cat years, I'd be over two thousand years old.'

Amethyst laughed. 'Basically, we're also ancient.'

'Ah. I see. Sorry. Neither of you look a day over forty, if that makes you feel any better.' Maggie shrugged sheepishly.

'It does a little.' Emerald sighed, her fingers still clawing at the table.

'Even if *that* demon is alive and well, it doesn't mean he's here.' Amethyst massaged her sister's shoulders and then gave them a reassuring wiggle.

'You're right. You're definitely right,' said Emerald.

A small and uncertain smile crept on to her lips, and she took Amethyst's steady hand from her shoulder in her quivering fingers and patted it several times.

'But we should investigate, shouldn't we? Make one hundred per cent certain it's not . . . *him*,' she whispered, not even able to bring herself to say his name. 'Whatever it may be, there's certainly something evil here in Crowood Peak, and we need to keep this town safe.'

'Of course, sister. We'll do a little bit of investigating to make sure there's no trouble afoot, but, until then, how about a nice cup of tea and a pastry?'

Just the word 'pastry' made Emerald visibly relax, her shoulders dropping and the creases in her forehead smoothing out. Spending three hundred years as a cat meant that she'd not only missed out on eating human food but also on trying all the new and yummy things that hadn't even existed when she was last walking around on two legs. Her favourite so far was the Danish pastry.

'You do realize what this is, right?' Maggie hopped from foot to foot, unable to contain her excitement. Ivy, Emerald and Amethyst all looked at her expectantly. 'This is a job for –' Maggie ran up the stepladder and threw her arms in the air – 'THE DOUBLE TROUBLE SOCIETY!'

It would have been a triumphant moment had she not accidentally punched a cupboard door, causing it to fall clean off its hinges.

'Whoops. Sorry . . . !'

3
First Day of School

Coming up with a plan of action was going to have to wait. The summer was finally over, and it was time for Maggie and Ivy to return to school. Something they had widely differing feelings about.

'I can't *wait* to get back to lessons. I've heard a rumour that we've got Miss Snow for art this year, and that she gives everyone orange sweets at the end of class.' Ivy was ready for the exciting day ahead, her bag neatly packed with all her new books and stationery.

'Knowing my rotten luck, we'll end up with Mad Mr Munster for maths again this year. He's definitely got it in for me,' Maggie said crossly as she tied, untied and retied her shoes.

'Only because you spend most of his lessons doodling in your notebook instead of actually listening to him. I quite like him. He gives me extra homework.' Ivy grinned, puffing out her chest proudly.

'I am a town hero! Town heroes shouldn't get extra homework. They should be given flowers and . . . and . . . as many biscuits as they want!' Maggie produced a chocolate biscuit from her pocket and put the entire thing in her mouth so that her cheeks bulged out like a hamster.

'Now, now, Maggie.' Max appeared in the hallway, holding out two lunch boxes, one pink and one green. 'Let's not be big-headed about what happened at the festival. What you did was amazing, of course, but that doesn't get you out of going to school and learning all the same important lessons as everyone else. You're special and brilliant, but so is everyone in their own unique way. We all get our time to shine eventually. Yours just happened to be a little more . . . magical than most.'

'Not to mention terrifying!' Bill appeared in the hallway behind Max, drying his hands on a tea towel.

Maggie and Max and Bill and Ivy had always been close, but after Bill and Max were turned into stone statues they'd all been spending a lot more time together, like one big family unit. If they weren't at the Tomb household, then they were at the Eeries. And if they were at neither of those they were sure to be found sitting round the kitchen table at Hokum House, laughing long past the girls' bedtime, eating whatever sweet treat Amethyst had cooked up and watching Emerald turn from cat to witch and back again. Along with the new and improved Double Trouble Society, Maggie and Ivy had never felt so surrounded by love and friendship.

'Don't worry, Dad. I'll be sure to keep Maggie's big head in check,' Ivy said with a prod to the centre of her best friend's forehead.

'I don't have a big head!' Maggie folded her arms across her chest. 'I just don't like maths, that's all.'

Max laughed. 'Well, for the sake of the Tomb family, one of us has to be good at it, and it certainly isn't me.'

'I can always help, Max. You should have said! Let's go over some simple fractions today at lunch. I've got some advanced mathematics books upstairs. I'll go and fetch them. Oh brilliant! I thought today was going to be a bit boring, but now it's shaping up to be the most thrilling day of the week!'

Bill rubbed his hands together and leaped up the stairs two at a time. Max, however, was looking a little pale.

'Did I . . . just voluntarily sign up for maths lessons?' he said, staring wide-eyed up the stairs after Bill.

'Yes, Dad. I think you did,' Maggie said, unable to stifle her laughter.

'Don't worry. I'm sure he'll go easy on you.' Ivy patted Max on the arm reassuringly and then bounced out of the front door.

Max grabbed Maggie's hand just as she was about to follow.

'Have I still got time to hide, do you reckon?' he whispered just as Bill appeared at the top of the stairs with a teetering pile of maths textbooks in his arms.

'Sorry, Dad. I think you're also going to school today.' Maggie slipped her hand out from her father's, held her thumb to her nose and wiggled her fingers. 'Looks like you've got to be the maths whizz of the family now!' And she ran out of the house, giggling.

After the last blue moon in Crowood Peak, Maggie and Ivy's route to school became much longer as there were new members of the Double Trouble Society to collect along the way. It meant getting up a little earlier, but they didn't mind because they were the leaders of the society, after all. First they stopped off at Eddie's house. He was usually up the earliest and often liked to review the previous night's homework with Ivy on the way to school. Sometimes they'd test each other on spelling, equations or the dates of important events in history.

'Can you imagine what it's going to be like when we finally get to go to university?' Ivy said wistfully.

'When we finally feel a little more intellectually challenged, you mean?' Eddie said with a sigh.

'Now, now, Eddie. No one likes a big-head. There's still a lot we can learn in school. Especially with two real-life witches in town. Just imagine when we know how to make actual potions?!' Ivy clapped her hands together excitedly.

No one outside Crowood Peak knew about the witches or that the town was now filled with magic. Nobody really paid attention to such a small and unimportant place, anyway, but the witches had cast a few spells to make sure that no hint of magic ever made it beyond Crowood's boundaries. They'd had enough trouble with some of the town's inhabitants being unhappy that they lived there. It was vital to keep the magic a secret, or people from all over would be clamouring to get their problems fixed by the witches.

'I don't understand how you two have your whole lives planned out already,' said Maggie, laughing. She removed her headphones, letting them dangle round her neck. 'Don't you just want to . . . y'know . . . go with the flow?' She made her arms and legs go all floppy and did a little jelly-legged jig for them.

'I don't enjoy surprises. I like to know exactly what's going to happen and when,' said Eddie.

'Me too. That's why we're going to apply to the same college and the same university, and then we're going to start our own inventions company.' Ivy stared off into the middle distance, picturing it all.

‘And where exactly do I fit into all this?’ said Maggie in a small voice.

‘You’ll be busy writing bestselling novels! And then, when we get free time, you and I can come back here to visit Dad and Max and Frankenstein.’

Frankenstein was Maggie’s excitable dog. When they’d first adopted him, Max said he looked like four different dogs had been sewn together to make this one dopey, lovable mongrel. So they named him Frankenstein.

‘Wow, you really do have it all figured out, don’t you?’ Maggie chuckled.

‘Yup!’ Ivy and Eddie said together, and they picked up their pace, testing each other on the birthdates of the Plantagenet monarchs.

Maggie did occasionally try to listen when Eddie and Ivy tested each other, but sometimes all those numbers and dates just went over her head. Then she would put on her headphones and listen to her favourite band, the Howling Horrors, or an audiobook. Recently, Maggie had started listening to ghost stories. After the festival, she’d discovered a taste for the macabre and, even though she’d prefer not to find herself in a situation where she’d have to defeat dark magic again, she still loved the thrill of it all. So, while Eddie and Ivy chatted, she listened to another album or another chapter and danced along behind them until they reached Isaac’s house.

Isaac had upped his game when it came to collecting weird and wonderful things. He'd turned his hand to taxidermy after his pet mouse had sadly died of old age. Since then, his obsession had grown, and he had found and stuffed dead mice and rats and even a crow that had crashed into his bedroom window and then landed on the patio. He never brought them to school, but he recounted every little detail of the process to Maggie, who listened in horrified fascination.

Next they picked up Jennifer, Jamie and Jemima, who all lived on the same street. Jennifer was amazing at making things and usually had something new to show the group, whether that was a hat she'd crocheted or a scarf she'd knitted.

When they got to Jamie's house, however, Maggie, Ivy, Eddie, Isaac and Jennifer would always line up either side of the path that led to his front door and patiently wait for it to open. When it finally did (fashionably late), Jamie would strut past them as if he was on a catwalk in Milan or Paris, his guitar case swinging by his side. Maggie would take off her headphones and play her music out loud, Jennifer and Isaac would pretend to be the paparazzi, snapping pictures on their invisible cameras, and Eddie and Ivy would play the part of eager reporters, desperate to know what inspired today's look.

Jamie was not only spectacular at putting together an outfit, he was also amazing at making his own clothes. Inspired by Jennifer's creations, and after digging out his granny's old sewing machine and asking her for some lessons, he soon had a whole new wardrobe (although his mum had a few less curtains and bedsheets).

Today he was sporting his latest shirt. The left side was dark blue and the right side had white and blue stripes. He had on matching shorts except the left leg was striped and the right one was blue. He'd paired the ensemble with white platform trainers that made him stand at least fifteen centimetres taller than everyone else, and his brown hair was gelled up, giving him even more height.

The gang all whooped and cheered, and when Jamie got to his front gate he turned, posed and said, 'Well, aren't you coming?'

Jemima had been a little sheepish after the festival last year. Before it, she'd often been mean and spiteful to everyone, and as a result had not been around to help defeat the Crowood Witch and had been the only one in town to miss everything that happened. Once the others had filled her in, she felt simply terrible. She couldn't join in any conversations about the magic they'd all felt coursing through their veins, about what it had looked like when all the darkness left Emerald's body or how awesome it had been when Amethyst used the force of the blue moon to enhance her power.

After some of the excitement had died down, though, and when she felt a little less like she'd let everyone down, she started to come out of her shell. The spell Amethyst had cast to stop Jemima saying nasty things soon faded, but Jemima began to realize how amazing she felt when she was kind to people.

Now that she had softened, the Double Trouble Society really benefitted from her presence. She was witty rather than sharp-tongued, and she was tougher than any of them. When there was a hard or scary task to be done, Jemima was at the front of the queue, with Maggie close behind. Her bravery was second to none.

Finally, they collected Darla. Darla, who was only five, was often perched on the windowsill, wedged between her stuffed animals, waiting eagerly for her group of friends to arrive. As soon as she spotted them coming down the road, she banged on the window and waved frantically. She ran to the door with her dad behind her holding her coat, shoes, book bag and lunch box, which he handed to other members of the group while the little girl hugged everyone.

Darla usually held hands with Ivy and Eddie, and they quizzed her on what she was learning at school or encouraged her to tell them a story. Usually, though, she would just recount the tale of the festival the year before because it was her favourite.

One thing that they also all loved to discuss on their way to school were their dreams. Every night, Amethyst would cast spells with her moon magic, and everyone's dreams would be infused with the happiest of thoughts. Amethyst was an expert at getting the balance just right so that the dreams were vivid enough to feel almost real, but weren't so realistic that it was a disappointment to wake up. Instead, they made each person feel inspired to start the day and make their dreams a reality.

'Last night, I dreamed that I was the head of a huge fashion magazine that featured my latest clothing line,' Jamie said, clutching a copy of *Vogue*. 'And I also dreamed that my mum didn't make me play the guitar any more.'

'I dreamed my latest novel was being read by everyone on the planet at the same time!' Maggie said, skipping along the pavement.

'In my dreams, I got to fly to school on my unicorn instead of walking. I *hate* walking,' said Darla, tugging at Jennifer's sleeve to be lifted.

Individually, they felt like strong, capable and clever kids, but when they were together they felt as if they could take on the world. Little did they know that one day soon they would have to do just that.

4
Camera-shy

The Double Trouble Society had a new chant and it went like this:

We're no longer Double,
But we're Trouble nonetheless,
And we will never crumble
Cos we're braver than the rest.
We've got magic, we've got spells,
We eat the dark for lunch and tea.
We're Trouble on the Double,
We're the best Society!

They usually sang it on the way to school as loud as their lungs would let them while dancing round each other. The rest of their classmates could always hear them coming a mile off. Some rolled their eyes, others gave them high fives as they marched past, but the consensus was that the Double Trouble Society were now the coolest kids in school, and *everyone* wanted to be part of their gang. All except the three new kids, who looked on with puzzled expressions.

'What on earth is going on?' muttered Spencer.

'They look like they're having fun,' Harriet said, her voice tinged with a longing that she just couldn't hide. 'I wonder who they are.' *And if they'll let me join in*, she thought.

'You mean you don't know who they are?' Orville Thomas had been standing in front of them both, taking photos. He whipped his head round to Harriet, making her jump.

'Why would we know who they are? I've just moved here.' Spencer had a very clipped way of speaking, making everything he said sound rude. 'Everyone's a stranger to me.'

'I'm Harriet!' Harriet practically yelled and thrust her outstretched hand at Spencer so that her fingers were almost touching his nose.

Spencer just took a step backwards and said, 'Charmed to meet you, I'm sure.' Instead of shaking her hand, he grabbed the edges of his velvet coat and held them out to the side as he bent at the waist and presented her with a very low bow.

Harriet couldn't help but laugh in surprise (how many

boys of eleven would do that as a form of greeting?), but she also giggled out of happiness. No one ever really said hello to Harriet, let alone bowed to her. She just wasn't the befriending sort, but she hoped – with all her heart – that was going to change.

Just as Spencer dipped his head and lost eye contact with them both, Orville snapped a photo of Spencer's grand gesture with a deafening click. Spencer's head shot up, and he glared at Orville with a ferocity that sent shivers down the spines of both Harriet and Orville.

'Did you just take a photo of me? How *dare* you!' Spencer lunged at Orville's camera, but Orville darted left, then right, and finally ran straight towards the Double Trouble Society.

Jennifer saw the commotion and, with Darla still at her side, stood behind Maggie, who put her hands out in front of her, ready to ward off any danger.

'GET BACK HERE!' Spencer screamed, and he hared after Orville. Just as he was about to reach out for the camera strap around Orville's neck, Jemima stepped in front of him and placed her hands on her hips. Spencer stopped abruptly, lost his balance and fell backwards on to the grass.

'What do you think you're doing?' Jemima said, looming over him. 'Who even are you?'

'He was taking photos of me without my permission!' said Spencer furiously.

'I'm sorry! I'm sorry! I didn't know you were camera-shy!' Orville clutched his camera to his chest.

'Hey, look, this is just a big misunderstanding. You don't like having your picture taken, and that's totally fine. You've said you're sorry, haven't you?' Maggie turned to Orville, who nodded so hard his hair flopped over his eyes. 'And you'll delete the picture, won't you?'

'W-well, it's a f-film camera, so I c-can't d-delete it, but I will make sure n-no one ever looks at it.'

'See?' Maggie said to Spencer with a smile. 'No harm done. So no more scaring the new kids, New Kid. OK?' She held out a hand to help Spencer up, but he shook his head and hoisted himself off the ground.

'I don't know who you think you are, with all your loud chanting and bossing people around, but today you've made an enemy of Spencer Sparrow!'

Maggie looked at him blankly. 'Who on earth is Spencer Sparrow?'

'Ugh. *Me*. I'm Spencer Sparrow.' Spencer straightened his coat, ran a hand over his quiff to make sure it was still in place and stood tall.

'Ah, I see.' Maggie nodded. 'Well, that's OK because anyone who refers to themselves in the third person is definitely an enemy of the Double Trouble Society.'

Ivy couldn't help but give a loud snort.

'You'll rue the day you made an enemy of Spencer Spa– . . . of me.' Spencer swished his coat menacingly as he turned and stalked off, disappearing through the school gates.

'He was . . .' Maggie started, but was unsure what she wanted to say.

'Unpleasant?' added Jamie.

'Mean?' suggested Jemima.

'Rude?' said Jennifer.

'Different . . .' Maggie gave a small smile. Then she shook her head and turned to Orville. 'So we have some new kids joining our year! Awesome. I'm Maggie. This is my best friend, Ivy.' She gestured round at the rest of the group. 'And we are the Double Trouble Society.'

'Cool . . . um . . . great . . . that's . . . awesome and everything, but . . . I have to get inside . . .' Orville backed away from them as he was talking and then dashed off, tripping over his feet and barging into Harriet Harper's shoulder.

She almost got bowled over, but managed to stay upright and then noticed the Double Trouble gang all looking at her. She gently raised a hand to wave, then thought better of it, shook her head and trudged in through the gates after Orville.

'Well, that's three new kids who are all total weirdos,' said Jemima.

'Don't be so judgmental, Jemima. You used to think we were weirdos too once upon a time.'

Jemima shrugged. 'I still think you're weirdos. But you're my kind of weirdos.'

'That's probably the nicest thing you've ever voluntarily said about us, Jemima, so thank you.' Ivy laughed and bumped her shoulder with Jemima's.

'So we have Spencer Sparrow, the kid with the camera and the girl who looked like she'd stuck her hand in a plug socket. All new kids who are probably gonna be in our year.' Maggie counted them off on her fingers. 'I wonder why they're all so jumpy?'

'Are any of them Double Trouble material, do you think?' asked Ivy.

'Who knows. Maybe?'

'Not that Sparrow boy,' Jemima said. 'He seems like he's from a totally different planet! As someone who used to be a former bully, I reckon we stay as far away from him as possible. He's got trouble written all over him.'

'Oh no. Look . . .' Maggie tried hard to point inconspicuously, but the entire gang turned to look at once, and it wasn't very subtle. 'It's the new headmistress.'

'Stern,' Jamie whispered.

'Don't be mean, Jamie. She might be really lovely!' Jennifer said, lightly batting his arm.

'No, Jennifer,' Jamie said, rolling his eyes. 'That's her name – Mrs Stern.'

'Oh . . .'

Suddenly Mrs Stern's eyes were upon them, and collectively they couldn't help but shudder. Her piercing blue eyes made them all instantly feel as if they'd done something worthy of detention when they hadn't even set foot inside the school yet.

They'd already heard the rumours about Headmistress Stern. That she was a force to be reckoned with. That she was strict and uptight, with not a fly's wingspan of space for any fun or silliness. That she was No-Nonsense with two capital Ns and doled out detentions like they were sweets. Even if you were a straight-A student with not a mark on your school record, Mrs Stern would find a way to knock your confidence.

She wore her dark brown hair scraped back so tightly that it lifted the corners of her eyes into a permanently shocked expression. Her bun was secured by two very sharp-looking pins that glinted in the sunlight. Mrs Stern was wearing a black pencil skirt, a starched shirt that was so white it was blinding and a matching black blazer. Even though she was already very tall, she wore high heels – presumably so that she could tower over the students and intimidate them into behaving.

'Ah. The *Double Trouble Society*, I presume?' Mrs Stern shot towards them, her heels clickety-clacking on the ground.

'That's us!' Maggie said with pride.

'Yes, I've heard all about you, and if you think for even a moment that I'll be putting up with any of your shenanigans, then you've got another thing coming.'

Mrs Stern made sure she stared at each of them in turn, and one by one they all felt forced to avert their gaze, unable to deal with such concentrated disdain.

'Just because you helped save the day once upon a time doesn't make you special in my school. You're just yet another group of children that needs to learn discipline. Understood?' No one said anything. '*I asked you if you understood?*' Mrs Stern said with more venom in her voice than a serpent.

'Yes,' they all murmured, and Mrs Stern left without another word. It was only as she disappeared through the school gates that they finally felt like they could breathe again.

'I take it back. Her name suits her personality just fine,' said Jennifer.

'Right, gang!' Ivy clapped her hands together to try and break the tension in the air. She was determined not to let anything ruin their first day back. 'It's the start of the school year. Shall we head inside? It looks like we've got some new challenges to face already, but when do we shy away from a challenge?'

'NEVER!' the others yelled, and together they ran through the school gates.

5
Spencer Makes a Bad Impression

Maggie had been right. Spencer Sparrow, Harriet Harper and Orville Thomas were not only new to their year, but new to their class. Spencer took a seat in the back right-hand corner of the room, fished out a book of Edgar Allan Poe poetry and began to read with an expression that said, *If you disturb me, I will hurt you*, and it worked. Not a soul came near him.

Harriet Harper had the opposite attitude and took a seat front and centre. She was ready to raise her hand for all the questions she knew the answers to and talk to anyone who wanted to chat. She had sat in the front row at her last school too, but she hoped the kids would be nicer here and not throw little bits of ripped-up paper into her voluminous hair. At the end of every school day, she'd shake her head, and the paper would fall like snowflakes.

Orville Thomas decided he wanted the best vantage point of the whole class, so took a seat right in the middle of the room. That way he could see everyone around him and would always be in the thick of the action, ready to capture anything on his camera at a moment's notice.

Maggie and Ivy sat down in the second row after saying goodbye to the rest of the society who were in other classes. Darla was in a different part of the school altogether. (The gang had already said goodbye to her at the school gates.)

Maggie and Ivy sat just behind Harriet, but Harriet was far too nervous to turn round and say hello.

Ivy leaned over to Maggie and whispered, 'Do you think we should say hi? To be polite. The first day of the school year is always nerve-wracking, especially when it's your first day at a new school too!'

Maggie sighed, nodded and then gently tapped Harriet on the shoulder. Harriet whipped round so fast that Maggie and Ivy both jolted backwards, their chair legs shrieking against the floor.

'Hi! I'm Harriet Harper!'

'Hi . . . um . . . Harriet. I'm Maggie Tomb and this is Ivy Eerie.' They all shook hands. 'Welcome to Crowood Peak!'

'Thanks so much! I'm a bit nervous, but I already think I'm really gonna like it here. I just get a good feeling from the place, y'know? Seems kinda chilled. Like nothing bad could *ever* happen here.' Harriet looked at them hopefully, and Maggie and Ivy shared a glance and a gulp.

'Well, I wouldn't say that exactly –' Maggie began, but Ivy quickly put a hand on her arm.

'Yeah. Nothing bad ever happens in Crowood Peak. Do you want to sit with us at lunch?'

She had expertly tried to change the subject, and it worked because Harriet's eyes lit up and even became a little glassy for a moment. She visibly swallowed her emotions down with some effort.

'Yes, please. I'd love that. Thank you, Ivy. And you, Maggie. That's really kind of you both,' she said quietly.

'We'll see you at lunch then,' said Ivy.

Miss Lightfoot drifted in through the doorway. 'Good morning, moonbeams!' she trilled. 'Shall we find out what delights the day has in store for us?'

If Halloween was a person, it would be Miss Lightfoot. Round her black hair she wore a black headscarf that was covered in skulls and a matching belt that cinched in her orange dress. When Maggie and Ivy looked a bit closer, they realized that the dress was patterned with hundreds of little pumpkins. She had on black-and-orange-striped tights and pointy black shoes like Amethyst and Emerald. Little ghosts hung from her earlobes.

She floated over to her desk and, as she spun round, she snatched up a piece of chalk and waved it in the air like a wand.

'I recognize some of you from my music classes, but I'm excited to get to know all of you better now that you're in my form. Something you should know about me right from the off is that I just *love* this time of year. Autumn. Fall. Halloween. Bonfire Night. Oh, it's all so orange and cosy and crisp and filled with cinnamon, spice and everything nice! But also, in our get-togethers at the start and end of the school day, we're going to find out about some fantastical creatures in the lead-up to October to get us in the spooky spirit!'

'Is she even going to take the register?' Ivy whispered out of the corner of her mouth.

Maggie chuckled. 'Doesn't look like it!'

'Today, class, I thought we'd read some myths!' Miss Lightfoot squeaked and clapped her hands together, unable to contain her excitement.

'Myths? Are they female moths?' said Richard Marsden from the back of the class with a sleepy yawn.

'No, Mr Marsden. Nice try, though.' Miss Lightfoot gave

him a smile and a sympathetic tilt of the head. 'Today we're going to talk about the mythological creature known as –' she whirled round for a moment and when she turned back to the class she was sporting a set of plastic fangs – 'a *vampire*.' She hissed menacingly at the front row, making Harriet recoil in her chair.

'What do we know about vampires? Miss Eerie, I have a sneaking suspicion you already have some sort of list in that notebook of yours as you so often do.' Miss Lightfoot's hand hovered in front of the board, ready to write.

Without an ounce of hesitation, Ivy flipped open her pink spiral-bound notebook with a practised hand.

'Why do you have a list about vampires?' Harriet asked.

'After last year –' Ivy turned to a page of notes entitled Everything We Know About Witches – 'I decided to write similar lists for as many mythological creatures as I could. Just in case.'

Maggie and Ivy had written down everything they knew about witches last year when Amethyst moved in next door and they were both convinced she was a witch.

Harriet turned in her seat, her brow creased with worry. 'What do you mean . . . "after last year"?'

'Oh . . . nothing . . .' Ivy mumbled, suddenly realizing what she'd said.

'Nothing?' Miss Lightfoot shrieked. 'Ivy Eerie, I don't normally encourage an inflated ego or big-headedness, but I think your achievements deserve far more credit than you're giving them.'

'Thank you, Miss Lightfoot, but now really isn't the time,' Ivy said, looking directly into the searching eyes of Harriet, whose bottom lip was beginning to wobble at an alarming rate.

'Nonsense. It's always time to praise town heroes for saving us from dark magic!'

Maggie puffed up her chest with pride, but Ivy sank down deeper in her chair as Harriet slowly turned back round.

'*D-d-dark . . . m-m-magic?*' she whispered.

'Oh yes. The darkest magic imaginable. You're in the presence of Crowood Peak royalty. Maggie and Ivy here saved us.' Miss Lightfoot disappeared underneath her desk for a moment.

'Let's not forget it was with the help of two very powerful witches,' said Ivy.

'Witches?!' Harriet shrieked, pulling the collar of her leather jacket round her face.

'Whoops . . .' Ivy whispered. She leaned forward to put her hand on Harriet's shoulder, but there were so many thorns sewn to her jacket that Ivy didn't know where to start. Instead, she just said, 'Sorry, Harriet.'

'Here it is!' Miss Lightfoot reappeared with a bulging scrapbook. It was so full that when she untied the purple ribbon holding it closed it burst open, its cover thumping on to the desk under the weight of newspaper clippings, photos, ticket stubs and stickers. 'Now where is it? Where is it . . . ? Aha!'

Miss Lightfoot turned the scrapbook round and pushed it towards Harriet. The whole class craned their necks or stood up and leaned over their desks to get a better look, even though everyone in town had seen the newspaper article that was stuck to this page of Miss Lightfoot's scrapbook. The headline read:

Double Trouble Saves Crowood Peak!
Using bravery, cleverness and . . . MAGIC!

Underneath was a photograph of Maggie and Ivy hugging Amethyst and Emerald, relief etched on all their faces.

Ivy and Maggie watched Harriet's head move back and forth across the page, reading all about the horror and darkness of the curse that took over Crowood Peak last year. Apart from its ending, it wasn't a very pretty story, and Harriet began to shake her head as she dropped the scrapbook back on to her desk.

'I . . . I can't believe it,' she whispered.

'The story has a happy ending, though . . . I'm sorry – what was your name again?'

'H-H-Harriet Harper.'

'Well, Harriet, you have no need to worry at all. Maggie

and Ivy broke the curse of an ancient demon, and the darkness was banished.'

Maggie and Ivy both replayed the recent image of Emerald bursting in from the garden, terror in her voice as she yelled, 'EVIL!'

'Now, before we start talking about vampires, we have two other new students in this class, don't we? Raise your hands so we can see you!' Orville stuck his hand up, but Spencer didn't. 'Tell everyone your name, my dear.'

'Orville. Orville Thomas.' The class began to whisper to each other. Even Maggie and Ivy exchanged a look and a . . .

'It can't be.'

'Can't it?'

'Orville Thomas?' Miss Lightfoot crossed her arms and tapped her foot. 'Why does that name ring a bell?'

'As in . . . Orin Thomas?' said Tillie.

'You're not related, are you?' asked Freddie.

' Um . . . yeah. He was my great-great-great-great-great-great-great-great-uncle. My family moved away from Crowood Peak, and this is the first time we've been back since . . . since what happened to Uncle Orin.'

Even though Orville had been born three hundred years later, what had happened to his uncle all that time ago seemed to really affect him. He lowered his eyes when he spoke, and a hush fell over the classroom, everyone understanding without being told that this deserved a respectful silence.

'I'm ever so sorry about what happened, Orville. But you're safe in Crowood now. The curse has been broken, thanks to your two clever classmates here, and not only that but we have two witches in residence who have vowed to keep us all safe and sound for evermore!'

Miss Lightfoot clapped, and most of the class followed suit. Some even whooped and whistled. Maggie and Ivy found each other's hands under their desks and gave them a squeeze, knowing that they weren't as safe as Miss Lightfoot thought.

'So, vampires!' she said brightly.

'Hang on a minute,' said Tillie. 'Didn't you say there were *two* other new classmates apart from Harriet?' She pointed not so subtly at Spencer who was sitting behind her, still reading, but now with his feet up on the desk.

'Ah yes! How silly of me!' Miss Lightfoot looked down her register and found the name she didn't recognize. 'Spencer Sparrow! Where are you, my little moonbeam?'

Everyone's eyes began to scour the room for the classmate they'd never met before. When everyone's gaze had landed on Spencer and silence had fallen, he still didn't answer, but sighed loudly instead.

'Black cat got your tongue, Spencer? Come on now, we don't bite! We're not vampires!' Miss Lightfoot chuckled.

'Don't be so absurd,' snapped Spencer as he also snapped his book shut, which made the entire class gasp. 'None of you could ever be vampires. They're dark and fearsome creatures. You, *Miss Lightfoot*, are just playing pretend with those ridiculous plastic fangs of yours. You're not fooling anyone.' Spencer's voice was sharp and mean.

'I've never claimed to be a vampire, but even if I had I would expect my class to be clever enough to know that I'm not one.'

Miss Lightfoot might have seemed a mild-mannered, sweet-natured woman at first, given her love of Halloween and her devotion to scrapbooking, but she certainly wasn't backing down in the face of Spencer Sparrow's rudeness.

'He could do with that spell Amethyst put on Jemima last year. His words are definitely blood red,' Ivy said, scowling.

'Seeing as you seem to know so much about vampires, Mr Sparrow, why don't you give us a rundown?' Spencer immediately pulled his feet off the desk and stood up.

'Well, Miss Lightfoot, vampires are creatures of the night, but that's not to say they sleep all day. They don't sleep at all.'

'Then why don't they come out during the day?' asked Richard.

'They're allergic to the sun. They'd immediately turn to dust if even the tiniest ray of sunlight touched their skin. *Poof!*' Spencer blew on the tips of his fingers and then wiggled them through the air like the ashes of a vampire floating away on the breeze. A shiver ran down everyone's spine, and the hairs on their arms and necks stood on end.

'What else, Mr Sparrow?' Miss Lightfoot folded her arms across her chest, but she was smiling and nodding, clearly impressed with Spencer's knowledge of this particular creepy creature. 'Let's see if what you've got in your head matches whatever Ivy here has in her notebook.'

Ivy ticked off everything Spencer had offered from her list:

Nocturnal ☑
Never sleep ☑
Allergic to the sun ☑

'They can't see their own reflection,' Spencer continued. Ivy ticked that off her list too. 'Which means a vampire will nearly always look unkempt and shabby because they can never check their appearance in a mirror.' He ran a hand over his neat quiff with a small proud smile.

'And?' Miss Lightfoot prompted him, but Spencer didn't even have to think about what came next on his list.

'They can't be captured on camera.' Ivy ticked that off her list too. 'There has never been a single photo of a vampire in the history of photographs.'

Miss Lightfoot opened her mouth to ask for another fact, but Spencer beat her to it.

'They drink blood, they can morph into bats, they can't touch silver, they love garlic, they have heightened senses so they can stalk their prey with deadly accuracy, and most importantly . . . they're immortal.' Ivy continued to tick items off her list except for one. *Garlic.* She was about to ask Spencer about this when Miss Lightfoot interrupted her train of thought.

'Why is immortality the most important thing on your very comprehensive list, Mr Sparrow?'

'Doesn't everyone want to live forever? Wasn't that the aim of your precious little Crowood Witch?'

'How do you know about her?' asked Ivy.

'You've gotta be kidding me!' Spencer chuckled darkly. 'You just have to put a toe into Crowood Peak and there's someone telling you about what happened last year, whether they're proud of it or disgusted by it. Not everyone loves the witches, y'know? Especially the one that tried to eat someone's heart!'

'Her name is Emerald,' Maggie said and clenched her fists under the desk.

'Oh, the feline has a name, does it?' hissed Spencer.

'Now, now, that's enough,' said Miss Lightfoot. 'Sit down, please, Mr Sparrow.'

Spencer glared at Maggie and, when she didn't look away, he growled something under his breath and sat down.

'Now I'm impressed by your knowledge of vampires, but maybe we should move on to a different creature. How about werewolves?'

'NO!' Harriet yelped. 'No more! Please, no more. I don't think I can take it.'

'Not very fond of the macabre, Miss –' Miss Lightfoot consulted her register again – 'Harper?'

'Not really, no. Not my thing. At all. Not even a little bit.' Harriet shook her head so hard, her wild hair caught on the thorns sewn on to her jacket shoulders.

'That's a shame. Well, maybe I'll tone down my love of the dark a little bit for now, but be prepared for a *bit* more of this sort of thing in the lead-up to Halloween.'

Harriet didn't protest, but continued to look a little spooked by the mention of Halloween. Just then, the bell rang. Before Miss Lightfoot could say any more on the matter, the squeak of chairs against the wooden floor and the jangle of locker keys sounded.

'Remember, moonbeams, this is a brand-new term! A new start! A new *you*! So think about who it is you want to be. How you want to be remembered when this year is over. I know you all have good hearts and bright brains, so use them to the best of your abilities. Kindness is key!'

'She'll be saying, "Live, Laugh, Love" in a minute.' Ivy chuckled, but Maggie didn't join in. She was staring at the cover of Spencer's Edgar Allan Poe book that was back up and unmoving in front of his face again.

'Don't mind him. He's probably just nervous about his first day at a new school, and this is how he hides it. Let's use our "good hearts", as Miss Lightfoot would say, and give him the benefit of the doubt for now, eh? He might be one of our best friends before the year's out. He might even be part of the Double Trouble Society one day!'

'Over my dead body!' Maggie said, turning to Ivy, but when she turned back, not a moment later, Spencer was towering over her.

'No, no, Maggie. Over *yours*.'

6
Orville Has a Problem

'I bet you all my pocket money that Spencer Sparrow is the source of the evil that Emerald can sense,' Maggie said, slamming down her green lunch box on their usual table in the lunch hall. Ivy flinched at the noise.

'Maggie, you can't just accuse people of being demons. Spencer is just a normal kid like the rest of us.' Ivy gave a shrug, but began to wring her hands under the desk.

'If I can't be sure he's a demon, then you can't be sure he's not a normal kid.'

'By that logic, we could claim that literally anyone is a demon. We'd need to do a lot of digging and find hard evidence if we're going to tell Amethyst and Emerald.'

Ivy opened up her pink lunch box to find a maths equation on a sticky note on the inside of the lid from her dad. She solved it in her head in only a couple of seconds, but it took her mind off Spencer Sparrow for a few moments.

'Spencer has given us more than enough reason to believe he's associated with darkness.' Maggie opened up her lunch box, unwrapped the foil round her cheese sandwich and sank her teeth into it with ferocity. She bit off a whole quarter in just one bite.

'How has Spencer made you think that?' Ivy asked.

'*Heef offul*,' Maggie gobbled round her mouthful of cheese and thick white bread.

'Eh?' Ivy was puzzled.

Maggie swallowed, then repeated more clearly, 'He's *awful*.'

'So was Jemima last year, but she's not a demon. She's just a regular human girl.'

'You say that, Ivy, but I'm still convinced she's part troll . . .' Maggie whispered.

'Maggie,' Ivy warned.

'All right, all right.' Maggie sighed, defeated. 'But maybe we should do a little bit of investigating, just to be absolutely certain.'

Ivy groaned, knowing Maggie wasn't going to rest until she gave in.

'After all, wouldn't you feel absolutely terrible if Spencer *was* a demon and put a curse on the whole town, and then Crowood sank down to the depths of hell – all because we didn't do just the teensiest-weensiest bit of snooping?' She gazed wide-eyed at Ivy.

'Your imagination is something else. You know that, don't you?' Ivy closed her lunch box and pushed it away. Her appetite had vanished at the prospect of nosing around where they were clearly not welcome.

'I take that as a huge compliment. So that's a yes to the snooping then?' Maggie took another huge bite of her sandwich.

'The Double Trouble Society doesn't snoop. We investigate,' said Ivy, nodding authoritatively.

'Fine. Where do we start?' asked Maggie, but Ivy was already reaching into her school bag for her notebook and pen. She found a blank page and had just written Spencer Sparrow when suddenly a shadow was cast over the table.

'Spencer Sparrow? Ugh, that guy is the worst.'

Maggie and Ivy looked up to see the dark brown eyes and messy jet-black hair of Harriet Harper.

'Is it still all right if I sit with you?'

'Of course!' Ivy said, shuffling along the bench. 'We waited for you after class, but you disappeared down the hallway. I called you, but I don't think you heard.'

'Yeah, I just . . . I . . . I was feeling a bit weird. Needed some fresh air for a second.'

Maggie caught Harriet's stare and saw that, for the briefest of moments, her eye twitched. Harriet quickly busied herself opening up her black lunch box. She pulled out a sandwich that had such a big slab of meat in the middle that it was more filling than bread.

'What kind of sandwich is that?' Maggie sniffed the air. 'It looks like . . .'

'Steak,' said Harriet. 'My dad cooks a lot of meat, so I usually end up with leftovers for lunch.'

'Wow! What does your dad do?' Ivy asked.

'He was a butcher, but he's looking for a new job now that we're in Crowood Peak. My mum left us, y'see, and then my dad went a bit . . . Well, things got hairy for a second there. He's doing much better now, but we needed a fresh start.'

'I'm really sorry, Harriet. That's so rough.'

Ivy reached out and squeezed her hand. Harriet was so surprised by the kind gesture that she didn't think to squeeze back. She just stared at Ivy's hand on hers.

'What's all this about Spencer Sparrow?' Harriet gestured to the notebook and kept her eyes down, knowing that Ivy and Maggie were watching her closely.

'We were just about to make a list of things we know about him. Maggie thinks that he . . . he might be up to something.' Ivy gave Maggie a pointed look.

Ivy liked Harriet, but was she Double Trouble material? She wasn't sure yet. Best to wait and see if they could entirely trust her before they let her in on their plans, but that didn't mean she couldn't help.

'I don't want to sound mean, but . . . I get a really bad vibe from him.' Harriet shuddered.

'Me too! See, Ivy? I'm not the only one who thinks he's bad news.'

'I don't think he's particularly nice either, but I'm not about to go around telling everyone that he's a –' Maggie coughed loudly, and Ivy caught herself before she spilled the beans – 'that he's as much of a *nuisance* as you think he is.'

'Well, we know for certain that he doesn't like his photograph being taken. Did you see the way he almost ripped Orville's throat out this morning?' Harriet tapped the notebook, indicating that Ivy should record that.

'Yeah, that was pretty intense,' said Ivy, noting it down.

'We also know that he's obsessed with vampires. I bet he knows loads about other creatures too. He seems like the creepy sort that would know all about goblins and ghouls and werewolves as well.'

'Werewolves?' Harriet gulped and put down her sandwich.

'No need to worry, Harriet. There aren't any of those in Crowood Peak. We've not seen anything other than witches here – Amethyst and Emerald – and they're as good as good can be,' said Ivy reassuringly.

'Yeah, and they'll make sure nothing dark and sinister ever comes to this town. If it did, they'd banish it!' Maggie threw out her left hand, palm out and fingers clawed as if she was casting a spell. 'Or destroy it,' she added, flinging her right hand out to join in the spellcasting, 'and MAKE IT PAY FOR BEING WICKED AND TERRIBLE AND –'

'MAGGIE!' Ivy shouted.

Maggie was now standing on the bench, casting imaginary spells left, right and centre. Most of the other children were watching her outburst, their eyes wide.

'Sorry.' Maggie jumped back down and sat at the table. 'Got a bit carried away. My point is, there's really no need to worry.'

'No, there isn't, but after school we should tell Amethyst and Emerald everything,' Ivy said.

Maggie nodded. 'Agreed.'

'After school, we run home. Not walk. *Run*. OK?'

'What's the rush?' Harriet asked. 'I thought maybe we could hang out? I've not been to the Cosy Cauldron yet, and I'm desperate to try their biscuits. I really love biscuits.'

'Oh cool! ME TOO!' Maggie held out her hand for a high five, and Harriet was so enthusiastic she hit Maggie's hand hard enough for the sound to echo through the hall. 'Ouch! I would be angry, but I like biscuits that much too, so I totally get it!' Maggie grinned, rubbing her stinging hand.

'We can't hang out tonight, Harriet, so can we take a rain check? We really need to speak to the witches about this.'

'All right,' Harriet said, looking more than a little crestfallen. 'I do have a question, though. I know you two are the main founders of the Double Trouble Society, but there are other members, right?'

'Yeah! There's Jemima, Jennifer, Jamie, Darla –' Maggie began the roll call.

'So . . . where are they? I assumed you'd all eat lunch together.'

'Well, that's –' Ivy began, but then she looked round the hall, unable to see the rest of the society anywhere. 'Actually, that's a really good point. Where has everyone got to?'

Most of the Double Trouble Society were in different forms, which meant they often filtered into lunch at different times, but they were usually all here by now.

'*AAARRRGGGHHHHHHHHHHH!*'

Suddenly a huge shriek filled the cavernous room and bounced round the walls, hurting everyone's ears. It definitely didn't sound as if it could possibly have come from a human, but then Orville Thomas appeared with his mouth gaping and a scream pouring out of it like a banshee. As he ran into the hall, he was tailed closely by Jemima, Jamie, Jennifer, Darla, Eddie and Isaac.

Orville knocked over three other students as he barrelled past them. He seemed to be making a beeline for Maggie and Ivy, his eyes wide and panicked, his camera held tightly in a white-knuckled grip. Just as he was about to reach them, he tripped, roly-polyed and landed on his bottom at Maggie's feet. Most of the kids in the hall started laughing, and Maggie hauled him to his feet by the back of his tweed jacket.

'Orville! Are you all right?' Ivy asked.

'*N-N-N-NO!* I'm not all right. Something's following me.' Orville dusted himself down and shook Maggie's hand off his shoulder.

'Where have you lot been?' Maggie asked.

'Trying to calm him down! He came out of the science lab looking over his shoulder every five seconds,' Jemima explained.

Jamie laughed. 'Then all of a sudden he took off at a million miles per hour!'

'It's not funny! Something is definitely following me!' Orville repeated.

'What do you mean, something's following you? Is it Spencer? Is he giving you a hard time again?' asked Harriet, picking up Orville's satchel from the floor. The leather strap had broken as he'd skidded to a halt at their table.

'No, it's not Spencer. It's . . . it's . . . I don't know what it is, but something is definitely following me. Aargh!' Orville jumped as Darla appeared at his side, offering up her unicorn toy for him to cuddle. 'Oh sorry, got a bit carried away there for a second.' He reached down and stroked Mrs Unicorn's head as the others continued talking. Darla smiled.

'Before we get to what may or may not be following you, I have a question,' said Maggie. 'When we met you this morning, you couldn't get away from us fast enough. Why?'

Orville looked from Maggie to Ivy, and then his shoulders drooped as he let out a sigh.

'Fine. If you must know . . . I'm a really big fan.'

Ivy laughed. 'Excuse me?'

'Spencer was right. When you move to Crowood Peak, you hear about what happened last year everywhere you go. You two are practically famous! So, when I moved here at the beginning of the summer and found out about the Festival for the Twelve, the legend of the Crowood Witch and how you defeated the curse . . . I couldn't believe I'd be going to school with you and might get to meet actual witches!'

Orville finally took a breath. 'I guess I just got a little bit . . . starstruck.' He shrugged. Ivy blushed, but Maggie threw an arm round him.

She grinned. 'It's true. We are pretty awesome.'

'Maggie.' Ivy rolled her eyes, but couldn't help smiling just a little. 'So, you're being followed?'

'Yes.'

'But you don't know who or what is following you?' Maggie asked.

'No.' Orville shook his head.

'But if you don't know who or what is following you . . . how can you know you're being followed?' Harriet asked.

'I just know, all right!' he snapped. 'I can feel someone watching me all the time. It's like there's a pair of eyes boring a hole in the back of my head. My skin prickles, and the hair on my arms stands on end, but whenever I look around . . . no one's there! I know it sounds totally mad, but you have to believe me!' Orville had got himself so worked up he was out of breath.

'Orville, did you hit your head when you tripped over?' Harriet asked with a high-pitched titter.

'We believe you, Orville. Don't we, Ivy?' Maggie turned to her friend, who looked more than a little concerned.

'Yes, we do. This isn't the first time something strange has happened in Crowood Peak, but we should investigate further before we reach any conclusions.'

'We're gonna need help,' said Maggie. 'I'm thinking . . . maybe instead of running home . . .' Ivy raised her eyebrows as Maggie's face lit up.

'We fly!'

7
Flying Home

Mr Woodman was the school caretaker and a good friend to every pupil. He always had a kind word of encouragement if you were down in the dumps, and he told the very best stories. However, Maggie and Ivy weren't running to his shed in the corner of the playground after school for a chat or a story. They were hurrying there for something far more urgent and much more exciting.

'Mr Woodman! Mr Woodman! We have a Code Twiggy!' Ivy hollered as they ran to his shed, pulling on their coats and tightening the straps on their backpacks in preparation.

'Code Twiggy? I thought we agreed it would be called Code Rocket!' Maggie said indignantly.

'Why would we call it Code Rocket if we're not flying on rockets?' Ivy asked, rapping precisely three times on the door of Mr Woodman's shed.

'Because we rocket through the sky. Duh,' Maggie said, shooting her hand through the air.

'But that's just confusing! We called it Code Twiggy because the brooms are made of twigs, and it's subtle enough that no one but you, me and Mr Woodman will know what we're talking about. A point that has been entirely defeated now that we've been talking about this so openly for so long,' said Ivy huffily.

'Was that exactly three knocks I heard?'

Mr Woodman was a short man with a big bushy beard that, coincidentally, looked like the end of a broom. Not a witch's broom, mind you. Just your ordinary, regular, run-of-the-mill broom. His beard had turned entirely grey over the years they'd known him, but his eyes remained as kind as ever, surrounded by deep wrinkles that had been carved into his face from all the smiling he did.

When the weather turned chilly, he wore a brown leather jacket that had embroidered flowers midway up the sleeves, which is exactly what he was wearing when he opened the shed door.

'Those knocks can only mean one thing . . . Double

Trouble! How are my two favourite students? Not up to any hijinks today, are we?' He had an open packet of ginger snap biscuits in his hand and automatically offered them to Maggie. She took two.

'Not hijinks as such, but we definitely have need of a Code Twiggy,' Ivy said, peering into the shed behind him.

'Wow. Must be serious. Nothing's wrong, though, I hope?' he asked, his bushy eyebrows meeting in the middle.

'Not yet and we're hoping never, but we need to get home as quickly as possible and walking or running isn't gonna cut it,' Maggie said, occasionally spraying biscuit crumbs as she spoke.

'All right then, if you're certain. But be sure to return them tomorrow, or Amethyst will have my eyes for earrings.'

Mr Woodman disappeared for a moment and then returned, holding two broomsticks. They had been made by Jennifer and enchanted by Amethyst and Emerald, and gifted to Maggie and Ivy for Christmas. They were both made from the many trees in Crowood Peak.

'A witch's magic is always strongest when they're at home,' Amethyst had explained.

'But it's not our magic,' said Ivy.

'No. It's my magic. But that lived in you two for a little while. It knows you both well, so it'll respond to you when you ask it the odd favour from time to time.'

'HOWEVER!' Emerald had stepped in then and put her steady hands round the tops of both brooms before Maggie and Ivy took off. 'You get one Christmas spin round the block and then these are to be kept in Mr Woodman's shed for *emergencies*. You hear us? These are the witch equivalent of a nine-nine-nine call, except *we* are the emergency services.'

'I'm connected to the magic in these brooms, so when they're kick-started, no matter where I am, I'll feel it and will come back to Hokum House and await your arrival.' Amethyst had spoken to them both clearly so that they wouldn't misunderstand the importance of the use of their gift.

'I'll miss these two,' Mr Woodman said as he handed over the broomsticks. 'I often come back to a very tidy shed in the morning. I'm sure they sweep up while I'm out!'

'We really should get going, Mr Woodman. Thanks so much for your help,' Ivy said as she mounted the broom. There was a familiar pulse of magic under her hands, as if the broom had a heartbeat that quickened when she gripped the handle, ready for flight.

Maggie got on the other broom, and her fingers prickled and tingled, like the feeling you get when you've slept on your arm all night long, but the tingling started at her fingers and fizzed all the way through her body.

Even though it was Amethyst's magic, which they'd accidentally borrowed the previous year, it was as if Ivy,

Maggie and the magic had become friends. This meant that each time they got on the brooms, it was like a happy reunion. The magic rushed to greet them with open arms and embraced them in a warm and excitable hug.

'Fly safely!' Mr Woodman waved at them as they kicked off from the ground with a satisfying *WHOOSH* that flattened the blades of grass beneath.

Usually, if Maggie and Ivy were allowed to go flying, they enjoyed every moment and made each second count. They would whizz through the air and try tricks and loops and spins. Maggie even once had a go at standing on her broom as it zipped along, but after a very big wobble and a very frightening twenty-metre plummet, she only ever attempted it when she was much closer to the ground.

However, this flight was not for fun. It was so they could get to Hokum House as quickly as possible and fill Amethyst and Emerald in on everything that had been happening. Their first day at school had been eventful, to say the least!

Maggie and Ivy kept the brooms at a relatively low height and stuck to the roads, but stayed above any traffic lights in case they turned red and slowed them down. The walk home usually took about fifteen minutes, but the journey by broom lasted less than three. In mere moments, they were gently touching down in front of the garden gate of Hokum House.

The witches were waiting for them in the doorway at the top of the long path.

Ivy's foot was the first to touch the ground, and in that instant Emerald came rushing towards them, her green dress floating out around her, her green hair rippling in the wind. She was waving a sausage roll around as she ran.

'Girls! Girls! Are you hurt?! What's happened?!' She grabbed Maggie before she'd even properly landed, the broom clattering to the ground as Emerald took Maggie's hands and inspected them and then prodded her legs and head and face as if she was a rag doll.

'We're not hurt, Emerald.' Maggie giggled as Emerald pulled her foot out of her shoe and inspected the underside, which tickled enormously.

'Then why did you use the brooms?! You can't scare us like that!' Amethyst said, joining them at the gate. Emerald took a huge bite of sausage roll to calm her nerves.

'You said we could use them if we had an emergency,' Ivy explained.

'Well, what is it then? You both look like you've still got the use of all your limbs. Unless someone else is wandering about limbless or mauled or murdered, I'm not sure I understand what the emergency is.' Amethyst folded her arms, her stern tone unrelenting.

'No one's hurt or dead, but we do have so much to tell

you, and we couldn't waste a single moment. You said darkness can spread really quickly, and we have some suspicions that just couldn't wait.'

'All right, all right.' Amethyst finally nodded, her lips pulling into a thin, almost invisible line. 'Inside, now.'

Around the kitchen table, brooms propped up by the back door, they sipped cinnamon-spiced milk as Maggie cracked open the biscuit jar and finally began to talk.

'There are three new kids at school, and they're all a bit suspicious,' said Ivy, opening her notebook, her pen poised at the top of a blank page in case she needed to take notes (and she almost always did).

'Suspicious how?' asked Amethyst.

Emerald dipped her hand into the jar and fished out four biscuits. One disappeared whole into her mouth before either Ivy or Maggie could reply to Amethyst.

Ivy and Maggie took deep breaths and told the witches everything that had happened at school that day – from Spencer Sparrow's strange behaviour to Orville's claim that something supernatural was following him.

'Right.' Amethyst's eyes flashed an even deeper purple for a moment, and Ivy and Maggie knew they were in trouble. Amethyst's magic tended to show itself in her eyes when she was feeling a strong emotion, and right now it was clear she wasn't happy. 'So we've got a boy who's paranoid, a girl who jumps at shadows and another boy that you just don't like very much.' She stood up and folded her arms. 'Girls, I'm really disappointed in you.'

'But, Amethyst!' Maggie and Ivy began, but Amethyst's eyes flashed again as she towered over them, and they knew better than to carry on. Amethyst would never use her magic on them, but disappointing either of the witches was as bad as being turned into toads, in their minds. Maggie and Ivy shrank in their seats.

'Those brooms are meant to be used in an emergency. An emergency is a situation in which you'd call nine-nine-nine. If someone's hurt or gravely injured, or a demon or a vampire or werewolf or goblin really did show up at school. Three new children in your class that you're a little unsure of is *not*, I repeat *NOT*, an emergency.'

Maggie and Ivy looked at Emerald, but she just shrugged and nodded her agreement with her sister.

'Amethyst is right. This doesn't sound like the sort of thing that warrants the use of magic. Those brooms might be a lot of fun, but they're filled with magic that can be dangerous in the wrong hands. Dangerous in your hands, if you're not incredibly careful!'

Emerald stood up and moved to the doorway to retrieve the brooms. 'I'm not sure what those children did to make you so suspicious of them, but I think it's best these brooms stay in our garden shed until you prove to us that we can trust you with this kind of magic.'

'You can trust us! Honestly, if you met them, you'd understand! They're really . . . shifty,' Ivy said. She jumped to her feet, ran to Emerald's side and put her hand on one of the brooms.

'Yeah, especially Spencer. I'm telling you there's something not right about him! Oh, please believe us! We really thought we were doing the right thing!' Maggie went over to Emerald too and gripped the other broom. 'Please don't take them away!'

'*Enough!*' Amethyst's voice boomed through the kitchen.

Voice amplification was a subtle kind of spell, but it had a great effect. The light fixture above the table shook, making the bulb swing back and forth like a pendulum, and the light swayed from the disappointed faces of the witches to the sorry faces of Maggie and Ivy.

'There is darkness in this town, and we don't know where it's coming from yet, but we can't assume these three children are responsible in any way. I'm surprised at you both. The Double Trouble Society is all about inclusion. You accepted us for who we are, and here you're excluding other children for being a little bit different.'

'But Spencer Sparrow is unkind!' cried Maggie.

'So was Jemima,' Emerald said. 'And now you're all so close.'

'That's what I said!' Ivy nudged Maggie.

'Shush, Ivy,' Maggie hissed, nudging her back.

'And now you're bickering among yourselves. Honestly, I don't know what's got into you both.'

'Amethyst, I think they get it,' Emerald whispered, seeing Ivy's lip begin to tremble. 'I'm sure you meant well, girls,' she said, trying to ignore Amethyst's sharp exhale. 'But even so, this is not what the brooms are meant for. So, until we're certain that you understand their real purpose, they'll be locked in the garden shed.'

'All right,' Ivy managed to say, but it came out all wobbly like her bottom lip. She let go of the broom, and Maggie followed suit.

'We're sorry. We thought we were doing the right thing.'

'Tonight I want you to go back to your own houses for dinner, and maybe in the morning we'll talk about this. But tomorrow you need to go into school and make a huge effort with those three children. Harriet, Orville and Spencer are new and, after what happened last year, you two have a lot of influence. You don't have to like everyone, but you also shouldn't make the lives of the ones you don't like miserable. Do you understand?'

Maggie and Ivy nodded, collected their school bags and headed to the front door.

'It was your idea to use the brooms, Maggie,' Ivy whispered.

'I know. And I'm sorry, all right? I really thought telling them everything we knew as soon as possible was the best thing to do. You heard what Emerald said: "You know how quickly darkness can spread." Wasting even a few seconds could be the difference between someone living and someone turning to stone.'

The two girls shuddered at the memory of both their fathers being turned into statues the last time there was a blue moon. Together they trudged down the garden path. At the gate, Maggie pointed towards her house, and Ivy nodded.

'Yeah, I guess you're right,' said Maggie. 'Time to go home. Amethyst thinks we don't like those kids just because they're different. She reckons we're being petty.' She sighed.

'Well then, we'll just have to prove that Orville, Harriet, Spencer or all three of them are worthy of our suspicion,' Ivy said, swinging her bag off her shoulder and retrieving her notebook.

'How are we going to do that?'

'Don't worry,' Ivy said, opening the book. 'I've got a plan.'

8
Ivy Has a Plan

'I think Spencer Sparrow is a vampire,' Ivy announced after tea as they sat cross-legged on Maggie's bed, two glasses of milk on the windowsill and a plate of biscuits on the green bedspread between them. Maggie had a biscuit halfway to her mouth when Ivy declared her suspicion.

'You what?'

'Don't look so shocked, Maggie. *You* thought he was a demon!' Ivy said, taking a biscuit herself. It was one of Mrs A's cinnamon cookies.

As the weather turned chillier, Mrs Anderson started to bake her seasonal specialities like pumpkin loaf cake and plum crumble. However, due to Maggie's biscuit addiction, Mrs Anderson always dropped off her first batch of cinnamon cookies to the Tomb household before they went on sale at the Cosy Cauldron. Even Ivy, who wasn't much of a biscuit eater, had to admit they were beyond delicious.

'Well, I didn't really think he was a demon. I just thought *maybe* that might be why he was so awful,' Maggie admitted.

'Oh. Well, I'm pretty sure he's a bloodsucking, night-crawling, garlic-hating vampire.' Ivy flipped her notebook open to her list. 'Obviously, I can't be one hundred per cent sure until we do some snooping.'

'I thought you said it was called *investigating*?' Maggie took a bite of her biscuit to hide her wry smile. Ivy cleared her throat.

'That's what I meant. We're going to conduct a series of tests to see if Spencer really is a vampire.'

'Tests?' Maggie sputtered biscuit crumbs over Ivy's notebook. 'What tests? We're not going to make him angry, are we? Because if he turns into a bat right in front of me, and tries to bite my neck so that I turn into a vampire myself, I swear by the moon that you, Ivy Eerie, will be the first person on my list of people to bite.'

'If all goes according to plan, he won't even notice, but we will need the help of the Double Trouble Society.' Ivy looked up at the wall next to Maggie's window where her green walkie-talkie hung on a little hook that Max had put up.

'Do you want to do the honours? This is your plan, after all.' Maggie gestured to the device, and Ivy unhooked it. She swivelled the knob to turn it on and then made sure it was set to channel thirteen.

'Double Trouble, this is Pink Pen speaking on behalf of myself and Gallant Green. We have a mission. I repeat, we have a mission. Over.'

Ivy spoke clearly, but not too loudly. It was only around six o'clock, so it wasn't late enough to wake anyone up, but she was more worried that Maggie's dad might overhear their plan and put a stop to it. Amethyst was already concerned that they weren't being kind to the new kids. If Max Tomb got wind that they were planning to conduct some tests on one of them to find out if he was a creature of dark magic, they'd be in Big Trouble.

Thirty long seconds ticked by. Ivy was about to give up and hang the walkie-talkie back in its spot when it suddenly fizzed into life. The voice that crackled through the speaker was Jamie's.

'This is Violet Vogue speaking on behalf of myself, Crafty Crimson and Rude Red. Over.'

There was a giggle following the last name, which was Jemima. They'd all chosen code names together, just in case someone happened to hack the line and listen in to all their plans. They picked a colour and then a word to describe themselves. Ivy was Pink Pen because she was forever taking notes. Maggie was Gallant Green because she was always ready to throw herself into danger to protect her friends. Jamie was Violet Vogue because of his love of fashion. Jennifer was Crafty Crimson because she was so great at making things.

However, Jemima picked the name Rude Red after Amethyst had taken all the naughty, nasty things she used to say right out of her mouth. Literally. Amethyst put them in a jar, and Jemima had been shocked to see all those bright red glowing words. As a reminder to be as kind as possible, despite her remaining fierce edge, she picked the code name Rude Red, and it still made them all laugh.

'We're all listening. Over,' Jamie said.

'We have a mission for tomorrow. Over.'

'What's the mission code name? Over,' Jennifer asked.

'Mission code name? Erm . . . er . . .' Ivy looked at Maggie, who quickly scrawled something on a blank page in Ivy's notebook and held it up. Ivy stifled a laugh and then nodded. 'Mission Fang-tastic! We have three tests to conduct tomorrow at lunch regarding Spencer Sparrow, so I need you all to be there as soon as the bell rings. Over.'

'Got it, Ivy! We'll be there! Over!' Jamie said excitedly.

Ivy hung the green walkie-talkie back on the wall and turned to a very confused Maggie.

'What on earth are you cooking up in that big brain of yours?' Maggie asked.

Ivy picked up her notebook and turned it round to show Maggie. Her list of facts about vampires was very long indeed, but she'd highlighted three of her bullet points in bright pink highlighter.

'We know that vampires hate garlic.' Ivy tapped the first highlighted fact. 'Spencer was obviously trying to throw us off the scent by saying they love it.'

'Too right,' said Maggie.

'We know that vampires are allergic to the sun.' She pointed to the second.

'Yeah, they turn into dust, don't they? I saw it in a movie once. It was awesome.' Maggie grinned, her eyes lighting up at the memory.

'And finally we know that vampires don't have reflections,' said Ivy.

'Poor vampires. It must be really hard to get ready in the morning. How do we test this out on Spencer when he won't let us anywhere near him?' Maggie scratched her head.

'Just wait until tomorrow, dear Maggie. All will be revealed!'

9
A Bite to Eat with Spencer

'Come on then, Ivy!' The Double Trouble Society, minus Darla, who apparently wasn't very well, were practically bouncing with anticipation by the time Maggie and Ivy arrived outside the lunch hall, closely followed by Harriet. The morning had dragged on and on, weighed down by the anticipation of Ivy's plan.

'So what tests are we conducting?' asked Jennifer.

'And why?!' Harriet chipped in.

'The suspense is killing us,' moaned Jemima.

'Who's this?' Isaac asked, pointing at Harriet, whose cheeks were flushed with excitement.

'I'm Harriet – Harriet Harper – and Maggie and Ivy said I could tag along. Just for the day. I'm not, like, part of your society or anything. I'm just a friend. I hope. But maybe one day I could be part of the Double Trouble gang? Or not. You know. Whatever.'

The speed at which Harriet spoke made her hard to follow, but everyone smiled at her, and she breathed a sigh of relief.

'Harriet's with us,' Maggie said, putting an arm round Harriet's shoulders. 'OUCH!' Maggie had forgotten about all the thorns on Harriet's jacket, and they pierced right through her green jumper.

'I'm so sorry, Maggie!' Harriet yelped, helping to untangle the thorns, trying not to pull any loose threads out of Maggie's top.

'I'm here! I'm here!' shouted Jamie as he ran along the corridor. 'Sorry – I had band practice.'

'Since when were you in the school band?' Maggie asked.

'Since this term. Mum made me sign up because she's getting sick of hearing me practise my electric guitar at home. She thinks if I play it more at school, I won't want to play it as much at home. She said it's *loud enough to wake the dead*!' He laughed. 'So come on! What have I missed!'

'Right. We need all the help we can get for these tests, which is why Harriet is here,' Ivy explained.

‘Ivy, why do I get the feeling this isn’t purely academic?’ Eddie said with a sigh.

‘OK. You all might think I’ve completely lost it, but . . . I have reason to believe that Spencer Sparrow is –’ Ivy dropped her voice to a whisper – ‘a vampire.’

There was a moment of silence. Everyone blinked once. Then twice. And then three times for good luck.

Jemima nodded slowly. ‘I knew there was something funny about him.’

‘Me too. He dresses like he’s from the seventeenth century,’ added Jamie.

‘Which makes sense because he actually *might* be from the seventeenth century,’ Eddie pointed out.

‘Wait . . . you all believe me?’ Ivy gasped. ‘I mean, I knew Maggie would, but . . . all of you? Even Jemima?’

‘The last time I didn’t believe you I almost got whisked away by a tornado of crows!’ Jemima laughed.

‘W-a-waait . . . what?’ Harriet’s voice wobbled.

‘I won’t be a disbeliever this time. I’m safest if I stick with you. You and Maggie haven’t steered us wrong yet!’ Jemima said with a grin.

‘Yeah, you’re our fearless leaders, and if you say this boy is a vampire, he’s a vampire,’ said Jennifer.

‘None of us really believed in witches until you two showed us a couple of actual spellcasters in our very own town.’ Isaac smiled.

'We'd be silly if we accepted the reality of witches but drew the line at vampires,' said Eddie.

'I suppose that's true. Thanks, gang. That's going to make all this a lot simpler.' Ivy opened up her notebook to show them her three highlighted facts about vampires.

'Our first test is all to do with garlic. Vampires hate the stuff, so we need to test whether Spencer will eat it or not.'

'How?' Jennifer asked, clutching her throat. All this talk of vampires had suddenly made her very aware of how exposed her neck was. She wished she'd worn that new thick, chunky scarf she'd recently knitted.

'It's simple enough.' Ivy pointed to the menu pinned on the noticeboard. 'They're serving garlic bread with lunch today.' She grinned mischievously.

'But what if he just doesn't like garlic bread?' asked Maggie.

'Or he's allergic?' Harriet chimed in.

'It is a possibility, but if he fails the other two vampire tests that I have planned, then we'll know he probably avoided the garlic because it would burn his hands and his mouth. Not because he just doesn't like the flavour.'

'Also, who doesn't like garlic bread?' said Maggie, looking horrified at the thought. 'It must be really hard to be a vampire.' She shook her head sadly. 'Missing out on all that great food. I mean . . . what if you're a vampire who lives somewhere like Italy or France where the food is *soooo* good, but they use lots of garlic, so you can't even try a little bit of *anything*. No wonder they go around biting people. They must be *starving*!'

Ivy giggled. 'This insight into the way your mind works is fascinating, Maggie!'

'Hang on. Do vampires even eat "normal people" food?' Isaac asked, his own tummy rumbling at the talk of garlic bread.

'Yes, they do, but it doesn't fill them up. They need to feed on blood to feel like they've properly eaten. So, if Spencer is a vampire and wants to blend in at school, he'll be eating along with the rest of us,' Ivy explained.

'Right. The Garlic Test is a go,' said Isaac.

'Good timing, too, because here he comes.'

As one, the Double Trouble Society spun round just as Spencer approached them, making him jump a little, but he styled it out and ran a hand over his neat red quiff.

'What's up with you lot?' He peered down his long nose at them. 'You all look like you've seen a ghost.'

'Not a ghost exactly . . .' Jemima muttered darkly, but Jamie and Jennifer were both a little too frightened of Spencer to laugh.

'Would you like to have lunch with us, Spencer?' Maggie nudged Ivy.

'After the way *she* spoke to me yesterday? You must be joking!' He gave a laugh that sent a shiver down their spines.

'Not joking at all,' said Ivy. 'Life's too short to hold grudges, and yesterday you proved what an asset you'd be to our group. Knowledge of creatures like vampires is invaluable to our team. After defeating a dark and demonic curse last year, who knows what might be lurking round every corner? We could always use an extra pair of hands.'

'All right then, Double Trouble. Let's see what you're all about, shall we?'

The Double Trouble Society collected their blue lunch trays and got in the queue for food. Maggie stood in front of Spencer, and Ivy made sure she was right behind him.

'So, Spencer, what brings your family to Crowood Peak?' Ivy asked, unable to look him directly in the eye. She had begun to feel a little ashamed that they were luring him to lunch under false pretences, but she reminded herself that if he did turn out to be a vampire then it was all for a good cause.

Spencer didn't answer right away. He was staring straight ahead at the protective glass over the food.

'Spencer?' Ivy nudged him, but he didn't react. She gently put a hand on his shoulder, and he snapped out of his trance with a jolt.

'Umm . . .' He shook his head as if shaking off a daydream. 'We're here because of my mum. She's an author and wanted to move somewhere peaceful and quiet. Somewhere nothing much happens.'

Maggie couldn't help but blast out a laugh. She clapped a hand over her mouth. 'Sorry! It's just . . . that might have been true a year ago, but now Crowood Peak is maybe *the* most interesting place to be.'

Spencer looked sceptical. 'Not that I've noticed.'

'Seriously? Come on. Two actual witches live right here! One of them can make the trees produce fruit that doesn't usually grow on this continent, let alone in Crowood Peak.' Maggie reached for a banana that had been picked just down the road.

'And no one here has had a bad night's sleep or a nightmare since Amethyst came to town,' added Ivy.

'Ooh, a well-fed and well-rested town.' Spencer wiggled his fingers in front of his face to heighten his sarcastic tone. 'Someone alert the press!'

'The dreams here are absolutely brilliant, Spencer. You seriously can't tell us that they aren't amazing. Most kids don't usually want to go to bed, but not here in Crowood. We can't wait to fall asleep to see what Amethyst has in store for us.'

Spencer chewed on his lip for a moment.

'All right, that's fair. But Crowood Peak is still a *sleepy* town. Literally. The best you can offer me is sweet dreams. You may have had a time of it last year, but nothing interesting's gonna happen here in another three hundred years.' He shrugged and slid his tray along the counter, a little closer to choosing his lunch, a little closer to the garlic bread.

'Oh, I very much doubt that . . .' Ivy muttered, only to realize that Harriet had most certainly overheard and was feverishly biting her nails. Ivy gave her a small, reassuring smile before turning her attention back to Spencer as they reached the main food section.

'What're you having, Spencer? There's fish and chips or spaghetti Bolognese today. I'm definitely going for the spag bol because it comes with garlic bread.'

Ivy watched him closely. She hardly expected him to run away screaming at the mere mention of garlic, but maybe a little eye twitch, a small bite of the lip, perhaps a clenching of the jaw muscles? No, nothing except a quizzical look.

'Good for you,' Spencer said slowly, eyeing Ivy suspiciously. 'I might have the same.' Suddenly he sniffed the air and grimaced. 'Can you smell that?'

'I can smell food, and it seems pretty great to me. Especially that garlic bread . . .' Maggie said pointedly.

'No, it smells like week-old rubbish bins and damp,' said Spencer as he heaved.

Harriet lifted her arm and sniffed to make sure it wasn't her. She switched places with Jamie at the front of the queue just in case.

'So what'll it be for lunch then, Spencer? Fish and chips or spaghetti Bolognese with *garlic bread*.' Ivy grinned as sweetly as she could, despite a feeling of impatience rising within her.

'What is this sudden obsession with my lunch choices? Have you lot run out of witches to hunt?' Spencer snarled.

'Just making polite conversation.' Ivy laughed, but it came out strangled and high-pitched. She took a breath to steady herself. 'I'm only trying to make you feel as welcome as possible in town. It's nice getting to know new people. We don't often get new residents here, especially not kids like us!'

Ivy usually found it easy to be polite. In fact, she was often complimented on her good manners, her pleases and thank yous, when she held doors open or offered to carry shopping for her neighbours. However, she found it increasingly hard to be civil to Spencer: he made it almost impossible.

'That's because my point about Crowood being the most mind-numbingly boring place to live is completely accurate,' he said.

'I like boring,' Harriet said quietly from further up the queue. 'I like somewhere that feels safe and peaceful. Not sure why anyone wouldn't.'

'Exciting people like exciting things, Harriet Harper.' Spencer's eyes flashed with menace. '*Some* people want thrills and adventure.'

'People like you, y'mean?' said Maggie.

'Yeah. Like me.' Spencer licked a finger and wrapped it

round the kiss curl that rested on his forehead. When he let go, it pinged back perfectly into place.

'Well, if you're such an adventurer,' Harriet said, not making eye contact with him, 'why don't you tell us all about your greatest and most daring adventure?'

Ivy and Maggie leaned back and shared a look. Spencer suddenly looked a lot less smug. Ivy squeezed her lips together in order not to laugh in Spencer's now slightly pink face.

'I just think, if you're going to criticize Crowood for being boring, it must mean you've been somewhere awfully exciting before here . . . haven't you?'

Harriet didn't enjoy confrontation, but she disliked people being unfair more. So even though her palms were sweating, and her tongue felt tied in her mouth, she wouldn't have felt right keeping quiet.

'Yeah, come on, Spence,' said Jemima in a sing-song tone that was unmistakably undercut with deep disdain. Then she stepped out of the queue so she could confront him properly, and everyone around them held their breath. 'Tell us about one of your many exciting adventures.'

'I actually . . . umm . . . well, I haven't . . .' Spencer stuttered, feeling more and more eyes on him.

'Haven't what?' Jemima put her hands on her hips and squared up to him. He cleared his throat and tried again.

'My adventures are forthcoming,' Spencer said, smoothing

down the lapels of his velvet coat and putting his nose in the air, but his cheeks betrayed him by reddening further to match his hair.

Jemima sniggered. '*Ahhh*. Thought so. Maggie and Ivy here actually have had an adventure, and a pretty big one at that. They harnessed the magic of a moon witch and used that power for good. They fought and defeated a dark curse that was three hundred years old. Adults ran screaming from the Crowood Curse and were turned to stone, and if it hadn't been for these two here, we'd all be orphans right now. And all of that happened in boring, peaceful, "nothing-ever-happens-here" Crowood Peak. So it's a bit rich to say this place is mind-numbingly boring when it seems you've got nowhere more exciting to compare it to.'

Jemima shrugged, and Spencer's cheeks reached the same colour as a stop sign. Except now he'd gone from embarrassment to rage.

'*You know nothing about my life*,' he growled.

Maggie and Ivy shared a look, but one of worry this time. If the test was to be successful, they needed Spencer onside. They needed him calm, complicit and docile. But he was shaking with anger.

'Spencer, what Jemima was trying to say is that –' Maggie began, but Spencer banged his fist on his tray, which made a loud *THWACK*. Everyone jumped back. He looked as if he was about to explode.

'I know exactly what she was trying to say. She was trying to say that I'm boring and normal and not special in the slightest.'

'Hang on, that's not exactly what I was getting at,' said Jemima.

'She was trying to say that I'll never be exciting or able to follow in my father's footsteps. She was trying to say that I'll never be good enough, but I already know that! *AARGH!*'

Spencer banged his fist on his tray again, but this time it catapulted into the air and spun over their heads, landing on the floor with a clatter that stopped the entire lunch hall. Spencer had lost his cool entirely. He ran, red-faced and shaking, from the hall on wobbly legs with Maggie and Ivy hot on his heels and the rest of the gang behind them. They chased him to a place where Maggie and Ivy could not follow: the boys' toilets near the science lab.

'Spencer, why don't you come on out and we can talk?' said Ivy.

But there was no answer. Ivy looked at Eddie, who rolled his eyes and made his way through their little crowd.

'I don't know why we're bothering when he's such a nuisance,' he muttered, pushing the toilet door open. Ivy held the door ajar so they could hear what was said.

'Spencer!' Eddie called, but again no reply came. 'Spencer?'

There was a moment of silence that felt endless to the Double Trouble gang, but it was broken abruptly by Eddie screaming, '*BAAAAAAAT!!!!!!*' Before he could emerge, a large black bat swooped through the doorway, squeaking aggressively at the group as it flapped its wings round the heads of Jamie, Jennifer and Jemima. Eddie reappeared from the toilets with his blazer in his hands.

He swung it in the air like a net in an attempt to catch the bat, but it was flapping its wings too fast and darted this way and that. Eddie kept trying and suddenly clipped one of the bat's wings, making it veer at once towards the ground. The little creature managed to catch itself mid-flight, but Eddie had made it angry.

Before anyone had even a moment to think, it swooped at Eddie like a dart heading towards a dartboard. It landed on his shoulder, bared two very large razor-sharp fangs and sank them into his neck. The Double Trouble Society all gasped in horror.

Ivy grabbed her notebook. 'Get off my friend!' she growled, and in one single swing she managed to knock the bat clean off Eddie's shoulder. It hit a locker with a metallic clang before sinking to the floor.

Faces suddenly started to appear down the corridor, accompanied by whispers of, 'What's going on?' and, 'Did you hear all that squeaking?'

'What do you think that was?' Jemima was bent double, breathless from trying to dodge being hit in the face by a wing.

'It was a bat, Jemima. Duh.' Jennifer was just as out of breath, smoothing her hair back into place.

'Bats are nocturnal! Being out during the day isn't normal,' Jemima said, pointing to the creature crumpled up on the floor.

'Ivy, Spencer wasn't in the boys' toilets,' Eddie said, swaying slightly.

'Are you all right? You look really pale,' said Ivy as Eddie stumbled forward a little, unable to keep his balance.

'I'm fine – just feeling a little funny after all that excitement.' He touched the place where the bat had taken a chunk out of his neck and winced. It was stinging pretty badly.

'The bat bit you, Eddie! You might have rabies,' Isaac said, inspecting the wound.

'The bat didn't look pregnant . . .' said Maggie.

'Rabies not babies,' Isaac told her.

'Hang on . . . if Spencer wasn't in the toilets, and we don't know where the bat came from –' Maggie said, piecing together all the fragments of the puzzle.

'Then that bat . . . could be Spencer!' Ivy finished her sentence for her.

It was at that moment that Eddie fainted.

10
The Vampire Problem

'W-w-we can't just skip school like this, can we?' Harriet whispered as the Double Trouble Society carried Eddie's limp body down the long pathway towards the school entrance gates. Maggie and Ivy supported an arm and a shoulder each, Jamie and Jennifer had his hips balanced on their shoulders and Jemima and Isaac had his feet hoisted in the air.

Harriet had the unfortunate job of carrying Maggie's backpack, which contained the unconscious body of the bat-that-might-be-Spencer. She held it at arm's length and prayed that the creature wouldn't wake up and try to fly off, taking her with it. Altogether, they looked like a very sneaky funeral procession. They all very much hoped that Eddie wasn't dead, but – more importantly – they hoped he wouldn't become one of the undead.

Harriet had to take big strides to keep up with the others. 'Can you slow down a bit?' she said.

'We have to be quick, Harriet. This is literally a matter of life and death,' Ivy whispered back ferociously. 'We have to get Eddie to A and E right now.'

'I don't think that Accident and Emergency will know how to treat a vampire bite.' Harriet eyed the two deep holes in Eddie's neck and reached up to rub her own throat.

'No. A and E as in Amethyst and Emerald! They'll know exactly what to do.'

'I wish we had our brooms,' said Maggie.

'I know, but we don't, and so we're just going to have to do this the old-fashioned way and hope that we make it on time.'

'On time?'

'We don't know for certain that the bat is a vampire at all, but if it is we have no idea how quickly vampire venom spreads. Eddie could be well on his way to becoming a blood-sucking night creature right now, and if we don't hurry we might not be able to stop it from happening!' Ivy's voice had started creeping higher and higher until she could hardly breathe.

‘Let’s pick up the pace, gang,’ Maggie instructed, trying to keep Ivy focused on the task at hand and not on what might happen if they didn’t get a move on.

The journey to Hokum House might as well have been a million miles. Eddie was only a small boy, but after five or six minutes the Double Trouble Society really began to feel his weight. Their shoulders ached, and their hands became slick with sweat, slipping against Eddie’s skin, which was growing icy cold.

By the time they reached the gate to Hokum House, they all wanted to collapse, except for Ivy who was running on pure adrenaline. She flung open the gate with a creak, ran up the path and hammered on the door until Emerald opened it. Emerald was holding the last bite of a brownie and had chocolate smeared across her face.

‘My goodness, you should be in school!’ she said, stuffing in the final mouthful. ‘What’s happened?’

The creases in Emerald’s forehead had been a permanent fixture since sensing darkness in the town, but one glance at Eddie’s lifeless form deepened them considerably. ‘Oh, Ivy,’ she whispered.

She wiped her mouth on the sleeve of her dress and swept down the pathway, casting a spell as she went.

Amethyst’s magic was stronger than Emerald’s when the moon was shining bright, but Emerald could draw her magic from the earth at any time without ever uttering a word. She waved her hands around as if she was wrapping an imaginary present in the air, and Eddie's body began to lift off the shoulders of the Double Trouble Society and floated swiftly but gently down the path and into the house.

Amethyst appeared in the doorway and had to dodge Eddie's feet as they whooshed past her.

'What are you all doing out of school? And why is Eddie levitating?'

'He's been bitten,' Maggie explained, out of breath and massaging her right shoulder.

'Bitten? By another student?'

'Well, possibly . . .'

'Possibly? Someone needs to start making sense and give me a straight answer soon or I'm going to get very cross.'

'It's hard to explain because you didn't believe us last time,' Maggie said with more fire than she'd intended. 'The thing is, we think we have proof of our reason to be suspicious of Spencer Sparrow.'

'Do you indeed?' Amethyst crossed her arms over her chest, her purple velvet gown swaying and shimmering in the midday autumn sun.

Ivy took the backpack from Harriet, who was still holding it as far away from herself as possible, and gave it to Amethyst.

'Open it,' Ivy demanded, and Amethyst unzipped it slowly.

'Oh my goodness! What is this? Is that a dead cat?' she shrieked.

'It's the bat that bit Eddie, and we have reason to believe that it is also Spencer Sparrow.'

'A boy who's a bat?'

'A boy who's a vampire!' Maggie snapped.

'And Eddie was bitten by this bat, who might be a student at your school and who might also be a vampire?' asked Amethyst.

'YES!' they all cried.

'Oh dear. Oh dear, oh dear, oh dear.' Amethyst turned quickly on her heel, still peering into the backpack. She muttered to herself all the way into the house with the gang trailing wearily behind her.

Jennifer, Jamie, Jemima, Harriet and Isaac followed Eddie as he floated into the living room and settled delicately on the sofa. A throw cushion plumped itself up and moved underneath his head before the full weight of his body returned, and he slumped on to the soft furnishings.

'Eddie's gonna be all right, isn't he?' Maggie asked, guiding Ivy towards the kitchen, where Amethyst had removed the bat and placed it on the table to inspect.

The creature gave a low squeak as Amethyst gently stretched out one of its wings. Now that the bat was still, it looked quite small and dainty. Nothing about it seemed ferocious when it wasn't flapping or biting. In fact, Maggie and Ivy thought it was even rather cute! However, it had bitten one of the Double Trouble Society and, as far as they were concerned, that was unforgivable.

'First we need to find out whether this is, in fact, a vampire or just a regular bat that got stuck inside your school,' said Amethyst.

'How do we figure out the difference?' Maggie asked.

'Well, for starters, this *is* a vampire bat,' Amethyst said.

'OH NO!' Maggie clapped her hand over her mouth and stared at Ivy, horrified.

'No, no!' Ivy said quickly. 'What she means is that the species is a vampire bat. That's just what this type of bat is called. It doesn't necessarily mean it's really a vampire in bat form.' She sighed. 'Eddie would have known that too.'

'None of that now, love. He'll be OK.' Emerald went over to Ivy and squeezed her shoulders reassuringly, but Ivy didn't miss the glance Amethyst threw at her when Emerald said it.

'It is a vampire bat,' said Amethyst, 'which only makes it more likely to be an actual vampire. Vampires can only turn into vampire bats because they suck the blood out of their prey. An actual vampire could never transform into a fruit bat, for instance.' She opened the cupboards behind her and began to collect jars. She piled them up high in her arms until she had to stop and tip them on to the table before they all toppled over and smashed.

'So a vampire could never turn into anything other than a vampire bat.'

Amethyst went over to the large pewter cauldron in the fireplace. She twisted open the lid of a jar, sniffed, nodded and then added a little of it to the cauldron. A potion was being brewed . . . but for what?

'OK, so how do we find out if this vampire bat is actually a vampire?' Ivy asked, impatience tinging her voice.

'The venom,' said Amethyst, adding the contents of several more jars to the mixture until it began to gently bubble and boil without the aid of any heat. Amethyst wasn't following a recipe. It was like her mind and heart just knew what to add to the concoction and, with every ingredient, the liquid responded in some way. It spat or hissed or sprayed or glowed.

'OK, I'm going to do something that may seem a bit shocking, but I promise you everything will be fine, OK?' Amethyst picked up the bat and wiggled it slightly into semi-consciousness. 'There we go . . .' she cooed as it opened its eyes a little. 'Ready?' she said more to herself than to anyone else in the room. Amethyst took the bat's head in one hand, lifted it and squeezed gently so it lazily opened its jaws and revealed two enormous fangs that looked far too big for such a tiny head. She then held out her wrist.

'Wait! No!' Ivy cried, but it was too late.

The little creature could sense the blood pulsing in Amethyst's veins. Its eyes shot open, nostrils flaring, and it bit down as soon as it felt the warmth of the skin that was being willingly offered. Its fangs slid deeply into Amethyst's wrist, and she winced, screwing her eyes shut. Maggie and Ivy watched as the bat's tongue darted in and out of its mouth, lapping up the bright red blood that was now oozing out.

Maggie recoiled in horror. 'Why is it using its tongue so much?'

'That's how vampire bats inject venom. It's not their fangs – it's their tongues,' Ivy said, scrunching up her nose as she watched the bat gulp over and over again.

'OK, little fella, that's enough now.' Amethyst pulled the reluctant bat away, even though it resisted. It tried to flap its wings, but she managed to prise it off her arm and lay it back on the table, where it instantly began to doze, its belly full.

'Amethyst, what if that vampire bat actually is a vampire? I thought if a vampire bit you, you turned into one too! Haven't you just taken a huge risk?' Maggie cried out.

'No, my darling,' said Amethyst soothingly. 'I'm not human in the same way that you are. If a vampire bit me, nothing would happen unless it sucked out all my blood and left me for dead. I'm a witch and will forever be one.'

'In the same way that a vampire is a vampire and so could never become a werewolf and vice versa,' Emerald said, a lingering look of disgust on her face.

'So what now?' Ivy asked, biting the nail of her thumb.

'Again, this might be a bit gross, but you'll have to forgive me and remember it's all for Eddie and so a very good cause,' said Amethyst.

She put her lips over the bite on her wrist and began to suck out the venom. Once she was certain there was none left in the wound or in her veins, she ran to the cauldron and spat it out into the mixture.

'*Ewwww*,' Maggie and Ivy said as they joined her and watched the silver, glistening venom swirl and sink into the lumpy green liquid as Amethyst stirred.

'What are we looking for . . . Oh . . .' said Ivy.

The mixture was becoming thinner and thinner, almost watery, and its colour turned slowly but surely from a putrid green to a violent red. The cauldron was now filled with what looked like bubbling, boiling blood.

'Oh my!' Amethyst gasped.

'I told you, sister. I told you there was evil in this town once more.' Emerald's hands had begun to shake as she put a hand over her mouth and whimpered.

'A vampire's not the same as a demon. Especially not *that* demon,' Amethyst said firmly. 'Vampires might be night creatures, but they're not evil.'

'No vampire I've ever known was good-hearted, Amethyst. They were created from darkness! Dark and devious magic!' Emerald's voice was climbing in pitch and becoming so shrill that Maggie and Ivy took a step away from her.

'Doris Dawson was a vampire and you used to love it whenever she visited, and you never said no to her clementine cake when you were little!'

'And, if Maggie and Ivy are right, then this creature could be a *child*. Have a little compassion, sister.' Amethyst moved the bat, still dozy and snoozing, to the centre of the table. 'Now, everyone hold hands and repeat after me.'

Maggie and Ivy stood opposite each other with Amethyst and Emerald at either end of the table and joined hands. Even though no magic had yet been used, the two girls could feel the pulse of it beneath the skin of the witches' fingertips as if it sensed that it was about to be set free and was poised, at the ready, just waiting with bated breath for the witches' say-so.

Amethyst and Emerald closed their eyes, and suddenly a rumble ran through the kitchen from the tiles under the witches' feet to the cupboards where jars and china cups began to rattle.

'*Sleep by day and fly by night,*
No bark but there's no worse a bite.
We won't be fooled, deceived, beguiled,
So, bat, turn back into a child.'

Purple light spilled out of Amethyst's hands. Green light poured out of Emerald's. Like snakes, the light slithered round Maggie's and Ivy's arms, and streams of green and purple wound round the bat's body. It began to lift up into the air, its wings limp. The light grew brighter and brighter until they all had to close their eyes. Behind their eyelids, they could sense the brightness fade, and the hum and pulse of the magic died out with an audible fizzle.

Ivy was the first to peek. She opened one eye and jumped back, breaking the circle, when she saw a large chunky black boot dangling off the edge of the table very close to her hand. Ivy's eyes followed from the boot up to the skinny jean-clad leg, the tails of a green velvet coat wrapped round a pair of arms resembling the wings that had been there just moments ago and then to the shock of red hair most certainly not in its usual neat state.

'Well then,' Amethyst said with a heavy sigh, looking down at the sleeping body of Spencer Sparrow, 'it seems Crowood Peak has a vampire problem.'

11
Eddie Changes

Eddie did not look well at all. All the colour had drained from his face and, when Emerald lifted his eyelids to check his pupils, the irises that had once been blue were now a dull and lifeless grey, and his pupils were tiny little dots, barely even visible. Eddie's body was becoming so icy-cold that it made the group shiver just to be close to him. They rubbed their hands together, blew hot breath on to them and chafed his hands, hoping to generate some warmth, but nothing seemed to work. No amount of blankets or hot-water bottles could raise his temperature.

Ivy began to sob. 'What are we going to do?'

'I'm so sorry, Ivy, but there's nothing to be done,' said Emerald. 'Once vampire venom has spread to the heart, no amount of magic can stop the process. He's transforming.'

'Is he going to die?' whimpered Maggie.

'Not in the way most people do,' Emerald said.

'What does that mean?' Ivy clenched her fists. Emerald and Amethyst shared a look and sighed.

'His heart will stop beating, Ivy,' said Emerald gently, and Ivy's heart almost stopped beating in that moment too.

'But . . . he will continue to live in the same way as before. He'll still go to school, be friends with you all and mostly be the same Eddie that he's always been,' Amethyst assured the gang.

'Mostly?' Isaac hadn't missed that very important word.

'Well . . . he'll be a vampire.' Emerald shrugged. There was no other way to put it.

'So . . . so . . . he'll have to bite people and drink blood and turn into a bat?!' Harriet shrieked.

'And he won't ever be able to eat garlic bread again . . .' Maggie shook her head sadly.

'We'll help him find a way to manage all the things that come with being a vampire.' Amethyst patted Harriet's shoulder.

'How long will he be out for?' Jemima asked, draping another blanket over Eddie and tucking it in under his arms.

'Vampire venom works quickly, but it may even be a couple of days before he wakes up again.' Amethyst put two fingers to Eddie's neck to check his ever-slowing pulse.

'A couple of days? What will we tell his parents?' asked Jamie.

'Well, as this is an emergency . . .' Amethyst looked at Emerald for her opinion.

Emerald nodded. 'I don't think you have a choice, sister,' she said.

'What are you talking about?' Ivy followed Amethyst as she moved to her spell-book shelves.

'A forgetting spell. I don't think there's anything we could say to Eddie's parents, any lie that would convince them that he's safe and being looked after.'

'If it was my little boy, and I was told he was going to disappear for two days, I'd demand to see him or speak to him before I believed the word of a witch who once wanted to eat the hearts of children,' Emerald said, her gaze dropping to the floor.

'Maybe just a brain-fog spell instead? Nothing long-term or damaging. His parents will just drift through the next couple of days, and everything will simply be a little hazy. They won't forget that Eddie exists: they just won't question his whereabouts. That way we can keep an eye on him here and be there for him when he comes round.'

'And maybe I could explain my actions to him too,' said a voice from behind them. Together they turned to find Spencer slumped against the door frame, rubbing his arm where there was a tear in his velvet coat. He couldn't meet the eyes of anyone in the room.

'All right, everyone. Let's remain calm and civil,' Amethyst said, but before she could even finish the sentence Ivy was racing towards Spencer. Even though he was much taller than her, she grabbed the lapels of his coat in her fists and shook him violently. Maggie raced to her side, unsure whether she wanted to stop Ivy or help her.

'Look at what you've done! You're a monster, and now you've turned my friend into one too! How could you?!'

'I didn't know! I didn't know!' Spencer whimpered. All traces of his former bravado and arrogance had completely vanished.

'What do you mean, you didn't know?'

'I didn't know today was going to be the day.' Spencer was now sobbing uncontrollably, his arms floppy and flailing by his sides as Ivy continued to shake him.

'Stop talking in riddles!' she shouted. 'You didn't know today was going to be the day that what?'

'That I finally got my powers.' Spencer's bottom lip trembled as he wept, and he screwed his eyes tight shut, huge hot tears pouring out from under his long eyelashes.

'You're a born vampire?' Amethyst gasped, almost dropping

her spell book. Spencer nodded and, when he finally opened his eyes and looked up, Ivy stumbled backwards in shock. His eyes were a burning, broiling blood red.

'Now, Spencer, I don't mean to come across as rude, but you need to understand that the safety of everyone in this room, including yours, comes first,' Amethyst explained slowly and in a gentle tone. 'So I'm going to ask you to back off and head into the kitchen. Everyone else needs to get behind me.'

They all obeyed except for Ivy, who remained in the space between Spencer and the Double Trouble Society.

'Ivy?' Maggie reached out for her hand from behind Amethyst's outstretched arms.

'I need answers,' Ivy said, standing her ground. 'If he's going into the kitchen, then so am I.' She calmly followed Spencer, who was walking with his head bowed and his hands shoved deep into his pockets.

'Ivy!' Amethyst cried, racing after her.

'Right, you lot stay here and watch Eddie,' said Emerald. 'He won't be going anywhere, but if anything changes in him just shout.' She turned to follow Amethyst into the kitchen, Maggie close behind. 'No, Maggie. You have to stay here and keep well away from Spencer.'

'No chance!' said Maggie. 'Ivy's my best friend. If she gets bitten, I'd only demand to be bitten too so that we'd never have to be without each other. So I might as well come with you. I'm not scared of stupid *Spencer Sparrow*.'

Emerald sighed and ran her long bony fingers through her green hair. She took Maggie's hand and together they walked into the kitchen to join Amethyst, Ivy and Spencer.

'Explain yourself.' Ivy folded her arms across her chest as Spencer took a seat, uninvited, at the table. He looked as though he might fall down if he didn't sit immediately, so no one said a word. Spencer looked round at the judging eyes of the witches and Maggie and Ivy before exhaling heavily, nervously trying to sweep his red hair back into place.

'My mother and father are both vampires. When they had me, they expected me to be like them right away. Except I wasn't. I was painfully human, showing no signs of vampire tendencies at all. So they decided to consult a specialist, who told them that sometimes when a vampire is born, and not created by being bitten, the vampire powers stay dormant until something awakens them. When we moved here, our clan was delighted to see the back of us. Thrilled to say goodbye to someone so unlike them. They didn't want me among them, and my parents found it hard to deal with that kind of shame.'

'I'm sorry, Spencer. That must have been so hard,' said Amethyst.

'So you're human?' Maggie raised an eyebrow.

'No. I've never been properly human. I've never had a heartbeat, and I've always survived on a diet of blood. But I've never been affected by garlic or sunlight. I've never been able to turn into a bat and fly. My fangs hadn't even come in until today. Which meant, when I did drink blood, I had to make do with the leftovers that my clan offered up from a cup with a straw. I couldn't even do any biting.' Spencer dropped his head into his hands in embarrassment.

'So what changed today?'

'I don't know. I've been feeling really weird since we arrived in Crowood Peak. I've not been able to control my temper. I've been angry at things I don't need to be angry at. And then today, in the lunch hall, Maggie and Ivy were digging just a little too much. I thought they'd discovered that I came from vampire stock and were asking too many questions. But this time when I got angry it felt like my whole body had turned into fire and, as I ran away, I realized I wasn't running any more, but flying.'

'You'd finally gained your powers,' Ivy said, and Spencer nodded with a smile, but the smile fell when he saw Ivy's eyes well up.

'I didn't mean to bite Eddie. I'm not used to these powers. I don't even really remember what happened. It's all a blur.'

'I remember what happened,' hissed Ivy. 'I'll always remember what happened.'

'Ivy,' said Amethyst warningly.

'I really didn't know what was going on. I just smelled blood, and suddenly my instincts took over.' Spencer looked down at his hands and clenched and unclenched them, clearly trying to get to grips with his new sense of power.

'Why aren't you trying to bite us now?' Maggie asked, looking him up and down and backing away.

'I . . . I . . . don't know.' Spencer licked his lips and put his hands to his stomach. It wasn't growling or rumbling, so he certainly wasn't hungry.

'That will be Amethyst's blood,' Emerald explained to them all. 'You fed off Amethyst not that long ago, and witch's blood will keep you fuller for much longer than human blood.'

'Don't tell the boy that, or we'll have a whole vampire clan on our doorstep wanting a bite and a taste,' said Amethyst with a sigh.

'I promise I'd never bite you or anyone. I swear on my life.' Spencer crossed the place on his chest where his heart should have been beating underneath.

'That doesn't mean much when you're not actually alive,' Ivy snapped.

Spencer nodded. 'That's fair. Then I swear on my grave.'

'Whoa, cool! Do you sleep in a coffin?' Maggie asked, wide-eyed.

'No, actually, I don't sleep at all,' said Spencer sheepishly.

'Aren't you exhausted?' As angry as Ivy was, she couldn't help but be intrigued. It wasn't every day you met a vampire, even if it was a relatively new one.

Spencer shrugged. 'You get used to it.'

'Hang on, why did you go after Orville that day he took a photo of you?' Ivy asked, remembering the first time they met. Spencer lowered his eyes.

'My reflection has always been something of a sore spot for me. A constant reminder that I wasn't fully a vampire. Well . . . until now obviously,' he said, picking up a dessertspoon from the worktop and looking at his lack of reflection in its concave surface with a smile. 'When Orville took that photo, I didn't know where it would end up. For all I knew, he was going to print it in the school newspaper or blow it up on huge posters and plaster them across the school. I couldn't risk my parents seeing it, or it would have just added to their disappointment in me.'

'How could you not have known you were biting Eddie?' Ivy mumbled, her head lowered. Her anger had now dissipated and been replaced by the huge wave of sorrow she felt at the loss of her friend.

'When a vampire gains their powers, it can be incredibly disorientating, and unfortunately terrible accidents can occur,' Amethyst explained.

'I've seen awful things happen when werewolves get their powers out of nowhere. People torn to shreds in seconds. So let's be thankful that Eddie is still in one piece.'

'He might be in one piece, but he's entirely changed. What if he wakes up and has no idea who any of us are?'

'That won't happen, Ivy. He's still Eddie. He's just Eddie with a few modifications. Eddie 2.0.' Spencer laughed, but, when Ivy shot him a look that would have killed him had he not been pretty much dead already, he stopped abruptly.

'Um . . . Amethyst? Emerald?' Harriet appeared in the doorway. 'I think . . . Eddie might be waking up.'

12
Barking up the Right Tree

Eddie was certainly stirring. They could see his eyes were moving beneath his eyelids, and his fingers were twitching. If they hadn't known any better, they would have thought he was fast asleep and having an awful nightmare.

'Isn't it too soon? You said a couple of days!' Ivy knelt down by his side and took his hand, which was so cold it was almost unbearable to touch and gave her the shivers.

'The venom of a new vampire is usually pretty strong,' said Spencer, keeping his distance and remaining in the doorway to the living room. 'So mine might be working twice as fast.' He touched his teeth, which would become fangs when he needed to feed.

'But it's only been a few hours!' Ivy squeezed Eddie's hand, willing him to wake up. His forehead crinkled for a moment, as if responding to her touch.

'Looks like I won't need that brain-fog spell, after all. I reckon he'll be up and about in no time,' Amethyst said, returning the spell book to its shelf.

'What about his parents? His very *human* parents. With loud beating hearts and veins full of delicious and delectable blood,' Emerald said pointedly.

'Ah yes.' Amethyst rubbed her temples. 'Well, maybe when he's awake we'll ask him to call them and say he's having a sleepover with the society. That way we can keep him here, and you and I can take turns being on Eddie watch.'

'Look! He's waking up!' cried Maggie.

The gang huddled round Eddie as his eyes fluttered open, and they all inwardly took a breath as his gaze met theirs in turn.

'I'm a vampire, aren't I?' he croaked, staring at them through his ruby eyes.

'I'm afraid you are,' Spencer called from his spot outside the group. 'I'm sorry, brother.'

'Brother?' Ivy murmured.

'Yes, I suppose that does make us brothers of sorts now.' Eddie nodded and sat himself up.

'How did you know you're a vampire?' Jennifer asked.

'I remember all of it. Every agonizing second. Your venom is . . . quite something.' Eddie rubbed his head and squeezed his eyes shut as if he had brain freeze.

Spencer chuckled. 'I'm not sure whether that was a compliment or an insult.'

'An insult. Definitely an insult,' said Eddie and laughed wearily.

'Fair enough. I guess I deserve that at the very least.'

'Eddie, you seem awfully calm about all this.' Ivy put her hands on her hips, unable to hide her annoyance. Eddie just shrugged.

'Well, there's nothing much I can do about this situation, is there?' He turned to the witches, but there was no hope in his eyes. He already knew what their answer would be.

'No, I'm afraid not, Eddie. This is a permanent change that cannot be reversed,' Emerald said gently.

'Again, I'm really sorry. I didn't mean for this to happen.' Spencer took a step closer, but Eddie held up his hand.

'It's OK. It's definitely unfortunate, and my parents are going to have a lot of questions when they realize I never go to bed when they tell me to, or when I ask for blood for dinner instead of tuna pasta, but . . . at least I'm not dead. Not properly at least. They still have their son. Just not quite as he was when they woke up this morning. My only issue is that I'm going to be stuck in school forever.' Eddie rolled his eyes.

'That doesn't sound all bad,' muttered Ivy, and Eddie let out a proper laugh, but then stopped abruptly and sniffed the air.

'Urgh. What on earth is that smell? It smells like . . .'

But Spencer quickly cut him off. 'All your senses will be heightened now. It'll just be your nose getting used to everything smelling stronger than before.'

Eddie glanced round at the society members, looked back at Spencer and nodded. Ivy had noted the odd exchange, but her brain was too full of questions to take in anything else at that moment.

'Now that you're a vampire, you're not going to eat any of us, are you? And you're not going to turn as nasty as *Spencer*?' Ivy spat his name as if it tasted horrible in her mouth.

'No, of course I won't. I'm still me. I'm just . . . a little different now.'

Ivy nodded her understanding, but even so her eyes filled with tears.

'Come on, Ivy. Everything's gonna be all right.' Eddie squeezed her hand.

'I have no doubt that it will,' Amethyst said. 'However, it does concern me that Spencer's powers didn't emerge until he moved to Crowood Peak.'

'What does that mean?' Ivy asked.

'It means that whatever darkness Emerald sensed before

could be drawing out the powers of all the non-human creatures in Crowood.'

'That does make sense. I wasn't showing any signs of my vampiric powers until I set foot on Crowood soil. It just took a couple of nights here before things began to change.' Spencer dared to take one more step into the room, but everyone flinched. Jamie even got up and moved round the other side of the sofa, so Spencer quickly retreated.

Jamie shrugged. 'Sorry, mate. The sight of blood makes me pass out so, as much as I'd love to have eyes as cool as yours, I'd never be able to hack being a vampire.'

'It's OK. I'll stay over here. But I'm not hungry. Eddie on the other hand . . .' As if on cue, Eddie's stomach growled loudly and aggressively.

'What's that smell?' He sniffed the air, his senses sharpening.

'Blood,' said Spencer.

'I think we need to get all the humans capable of being bitten and turned into vampires away from this house,' Amethyst said, quickly ushering the children out of the room.

'What's that noise?' Eddie covered his ears.

'It's the sound of everyone's heartbeats quickening because they're scared you're going to bite them.'

'Don't go. I'll go. I can't be here. I'm going to find a way to eat something that isn't one of you.' Without a moment's hesitation, with a *POOF* and a squeak, Eddie was gone and a bat had appeared in a little puff of smoke. It looked at Ivy momentarily, and without being told she knew what to do. She ran to the window and opened it as wide as it would go, and Eddie took off into the sky.

One by one, each member of the Double Trouble Society called their guardians and told them they would be having a sleepover at Hokum House. Most were happy to leave their children in the care of the witches, knowing that the house was under many protection spells and that their children would be safe there.

Amethyst cooked up a potion in her cauldron designed to give off a fog that would rise up the chimney and find its way to the person the spell was intended for. In this case, it was Eddie's parents. He still hadn't returned home, and the sky was getting darker and darker, the moon already full and shining. Ivy and Maggie were at the open window in the living room, searching the treeline for any sign of him.

'See anything yet?'

'Nope. Just the trees and the full moon.'

'Full moon?' Harriet gulped. 'There isn't a full moon tonight, is there?'

'Yes, there is, which is perfect for me.' Amethyst appeared behind them and took a deep breath, as if she was literally drinking in the powers of the moon. 'It means that this potion for Eddie's parents will be potent and will go without a hitch.'

'I . . . um . . . I think maybe I should get home,' Harriet said as she fumbled for her school bag and stuffed her things inside haphazardly.

'What? Why?' Maggie turned to help her pick up a book that had fallen by her feet. 'We were all going to watch a movie together and take it in turns to make sure Eddie and Spencer don't bite anyone.'

'As fun as that sounds,' said Harriet, as if nothing had ever sounded less fun to her in her life, 'I think my parents might freak out if I stay over. They don't really like me having sleepovers.' She could barely keep from trembling, and her eyes kept darting back to the sky through the window. 'I'll see you at school tomorrow!'

She snatched her schoolbook from Maggie and ran as fast as her boots would carry her, out of the front door and down the path, her hair streaming in the wind as she went.

'That was weird . . .' Ivy said, going to shut the front door that Harriet had left wide open in her hurry to escape.

'Was it?' Maggie folded her arms across her chest when Ivy came back.

'What do you mean, Maggie?' Amethyst pushed the living-room door to, so that the rest of the gang eating dinner in the kitchen wouldn't overhear.

'Ivy, how could you have figured out Spencer was a vampire, but not figured out that . . .' Maggie purposefully didn't finish her sentence.

'Figured out that what?!' Ivy and Amethyst said together.

'Harriet's a werewolf.' Spencer's voice came from the doorway. 'Nice one, Maggie. I was hoping someone else would figure it out so I didn't have to out her.'

'What?!' Ivy shrieked. 'That can't be true. She's so . . . so . . .'

'Smelly?' Spencer said with a mock gag. 'Yesterday, in the lunch hall, I could smell wet dog when she walked past me. It was the first sign that I was getting my powers. Eddie smelled it too as soon as he woke up. I could tell.'

'And she just freaked out when we said there was a full moon. She probably doesn't want to stay over because tonight's the night she'll turn into a wolf!'

'So she's a werewolf! How did I miss the signs?' said Ivy.

'You were more preoccupied with Mr Fang-tastic over here,' Maggie said, and Spencer tipped an imaginary hat at her.

'Hang on a minute. We need to be a hundred per cent sure before we ask her. She might just not like sleepovers, and, even if she is a werewolf, we don't want to embarrass her either way.'

'Ivy, I think this calls for your trusty notebook again,' said Maggie, but Ivy was already pulling it out of her school bag.

'Werewolves, werewolves, werewolves . . .' she said, flipping through the many pages of notes she'd made. 'Aha! Here we are. Let's see if any of these things match what we know about Harriet.'

Ivy put the book on the floor, and Maggie, Amethyst and Ivy all knelt round it. Ivy read out the list.

Everything We Know About Werewolves

1. They fear salt.
2. They don't like wolfsbane.
3. They have long, reddish nails.
4. They get tired after a full moon.
5. A werewolf has no tail.

'Have you noticed Harriet always wears red nail polish?' said Maggie.

'Yes, but that could just be her favourite colour. Lots of people at school wear it,' Spencer called over.

'All the other things require tests. Tomorrow, at school, we need to launch Mission Howl-oween.'

'Nice!' said Maggie.

'Thanks.' Ivy smiled. 'Salt is easy. She wants to eat lunch with us, so we can just offer her some to put on her food and see how she reacts.'

'Amethyst, do you have any wolfsbane?'

'We don't have any in the garden, but you know Emerald could grow some for you in a heartbeat.'

'Great. Could you go and ask her?'

'Absolutely. I should probably check on everyone, anyway, although when I last left them Emerald was showing them how she could make all the pot plants grow to touch the ceiling. They were having a whale of a time! I'll be back in a second.' Amethyst swept out of the room, and Ivy waited until she was completely out of sight . . . and earshot.

'Maggie, I can't believe I'm saying this, but tonight we're going on an adventure.'

'What?! Ivy Eerie, I can't believe my ears.'

'I know, I know. But if you're right about Harriet being a werewolf, then tonight is the best time to find out.'

'Why?' Maggie asked, but Ivy didn't answer. She just pointed out of the window at the full moon.

'If you're right, and Harriet Harper is in fact a werewolf, she'll transform tonight. And you and I, my friend, are going to see it happen for ourselves.'

13
Someone Sends a Sign

'Why does *he* have to come?' Ivy hissed into the darkness. Maggie and Ivy, with Spencer trailing behind them, crept round the back of Hokum House underneath the kitchen window where Amethyst, Emerald and the rest of the Double Trouble Society were all playing games, waiting for Eddie to return from his hunt. It was well and truly night-time now, and Ivy was beginning to worry that Eddie might have flown too far away and wasn't able to find his way back. Or that he'd bitten something that had bitten him back and he was now lying somewhere, injured and in need of their help. Or maybe he'd bitten a hundred people who were all also rapidly turning into vampires at this very second! However, if she knew Eddie, he would be just as cautious and clever as a vampire as he had been as a human. Maybe even more so now that all his senses were heightened.

'Spencer has to come because we don't know where Harriet lives, and he'll be able to track her down using his highly developed sense of smell,' Maggie whispered back, signalling for them all to move forward.

They'd snuck out when Amethyst started drawing her powers from the moon and dazzling everyone with how she could glow in the dark . . . Luckily, the one person who, with his super senses, might have heard them sneak out was taking part in the adventure, so it was easier than expected.

'Vampires and werewolves are said to be sworn enemies, but every werewolf I've ever met has always been rather lovely,' Spencer said, a little too loudly.

They both shushed him and gestured for him to duck beneath the kitchen window so no one would see him. Instead, he briefly turned himself into a bat and flew above the window and transformed back into a boy in time for his boot-clad feet to hit the ground.

'It's just the smell vampires can't stand. I reckon that's why everyone thinks vampires hate werewolves, but we only keep our distance because vampires have a heightened sense of smell, and werewolves smell like . . . well . . . wet dog.'

'Spencer.' Ivy turned round to him so abruptly he almost bumped into her. 'How can we trust you when the first thing you did when you became a vampire was bite Eddie?'

For all his swagger, Spencer really did look apologetic every time she brought this up.

'I told you. I didn't mean to bite him. It was an accident.'

'OK . . . so what if an accident like that happens again, and this time it's me or Maggie or . . . or . . . little Darla!'

'I think as long as I'm fed I'll be able to control who I bite. Remember that I'd only just come into my powers literally a couple of seconds before you turned up. It was just unfortunate that Eddie was right there. Wrong place, wrong time, wrong person. At least now I've got a friend for life . . . literally.'

He shoved his hands deep into the pockets of his velvet coat and left a little bit of distance between them as they walked down the pathway in front of Hokum House.

'Right,' Ivy said, sucking in the crisp night air. 'Come on then, vampire boy. Prove me wrong and show us why we need you tonight. Which way is Harriet's house?'

After a brief moment, Spencer rolled his shoulders back, stuck his nose in the air and sniffed hard, closing his eyes. When he opened them again, his pupils had dilated so that you could barely see any of his blood-red irises. Without warning, he began to move, swiftly and low to the ground. He wasn't running, but he was travelling so quickly, led by his nose, that Maggie and Ivy struggled to keep up. Spencer went ahead of them, through the front gate and out on to the street.

The wind was howling through the bare trees, making the branches sway. Against the light of the moon, they looked like clawed hands desperately reaching up to the night sky. Maggie shuddered. At that moment, a bone-chilling noise pierced the night.

ARROOOOOOOOOOOOOOOOOOOOOOOOOOOO OOOOOOOOOOOOOOOOOOOO!

'W-was that . . . ?' Ivy stuttered.

'A werewolf? Yes. It most certainly was,' Spencer said, nodding.

'Could that have been Harriet?' Maggie asked, running to the park gates to peer through the gaps in the metal bars to get a better look, but it was no use. All the lamps that usually lit the street at night were off. The park was closed to the public at this time of night, a giant silver chain threaded through the metal bars and secured with a giant padlock.

'It was either Harriet or one of her family. I very much doubt Harriet is the only Harper werewolf. I reckon she's from a werewolf pack, just like I come from a vampire clan.' Spencer picked up the padlock and jiggled it, but it didn't open.

'How are we going to get in?' he asked.

'Wait . . . you aren't really expecting us to break into the park, are you?' Ivy looked horrified.

'Ivy, this was *your* idea,' Maggie said, standing on her tiptoes and staring deep into the shadows. 'If Harriet the werewolf is on the loose, running round the park, surely it's not only our duty as her friends to make sure she's OK, but also, as citizens of Crowood Peak, to capture her and ensure the safety of –'

'All right, all right! You've made your point. We're breaking into the park. But how?'

'Don't vampires have super strength or something? Could you maybe bend the bars of the gates?' Maggie looked hopefully at Spencer, but he shook his head.

'That's not on my list of powers, I'm afraid.'

'No . . . but you can fly,' said Ivy. 'We might not need to break into the park at all.'

'Nice thinking, Eerie. Maybe I'm starting to see why you're top of the class.' Spencer closed his eyes and within an instant the boy was gone and a bat had appeared, flapping its wings and hovering in mid-air.

'Top of the school *actually*,' Ivy said, but she couldn't help but smile at the compliment. 'Fly over the park and see if you can spot anything. Don't be too long, though. If you're gone for more than five minutes, we'll know something has happened, and we'll head back to Hokum House and get help.'

'Amethyst and Emerald will kill us,' said Maggie.

'I know. Hopefully, it won't come to that. Just get a move

on, Spencer, OK? One quick sweep of the park, and if you can't see anything come straight back. Now go.'

The bat nodded and took off, flying higher than Maggie and Ivy had ever dared go on their broomsticks.

'See, he's not all bad,' said Maggie.

'You were the one who thought he was a demon!' said Ivy indignantly.

ARROOOOOOOOOOOOOOOOOOOOOOOOO OOOOOOOOOOOOOOOOOO!

'And, as it turns out, I was right,' Maggie said with a smirk.

'He's not a demon, he's a vampire.' Ivy leaned her back against the park gates.

Maggie shrugged. 'Same difference.'

'It's not the same even in the slightest! Vampires and demons are totally different, Maggie.'

ARROOOOOOOOOOOOOOOOOOOOOOOOO OOOOOOOOOO!

'They're both creatures that use dark magic,' Maggie explained, leaning her back against the gates too. 'And I reckon most demons wouldn't be opposed to sucking the blood out of mere mortals in order to live a little longer.'

'Vampires don't suck people's blood in order to live *longer*. It's so they can *live*. To them it's just a meal. One of their five-a-day. It's exactly the same as humans like us eating breakfast or lunch or dinner.'

ARROOOOOOOOOOOOOOOOOOOOOOOO!!

'Is it just me or is that howl getting louder?' said Maggie, but her voice was hard for Ivy to hear because overhead there came a ferocious squeaking. Two bats appeared in the sky above them. Spencer transformed back into a boy before he'd touched down on solid ground.

'RUN! It's here! The werewolf! We need to go *now*!'

He grabbed Maggie and Ivy by the elbows and heaved them off the gates. The second bat landed a little more elegantly and waited until its feet were on the road before transforming in a puff of smoke into . . .

'EDDIE!' Maggie and Ivy cried, throwing their arms round him.

ARROOOOOOOOOOOOOOOOOOOOOO!!!

The noise was now ear-splitting. Spencer, Eddie, Maggie and Ivy all covered their ears and turned towards the gates. There was still only darkness, but then their worst fears were realized. The darkness was *moving* because it wasn't darkness at all. It was *fur*. Jet-black fur.

Two yellow eyes as big and as bright as car headlights appeared and slunk towards them. The sound of claws scraping against the path sent shivers down their spines. Maggie and Ivy trembled, Eddie let out a whimper and Spencer gulped loudly. The huge creature hulked towards them, and neither Spencer, Eddie, Maggie nor Ivy trusted that the wrought-iron gates would be able to keep a monster of that size at bay.

'Vampire twins,' Maggie whispered, 'please tell me you have powers that will stop us getting eaten if that thing breaks through the gates?'

'Again, our powers are pretty limited to drinking blood and not appearing in mirrors or photos. We're not invincible, Maggie.' Spencer's voice was wobbling with fear. 'Harriet! It's us!'

The growling got even louder.

'Harriet! We're your friends!' Maggie pleaded. 'Why won't she listen to us?'

'LOOK!' Ivy pointed upwards. In bright red smoke against the black night sky, words began to appear.

With shaking breaths and whimpers as the beast at the gates growled louder and louder, they read the message.

A CURSE WAS BROKEN
YOU WILL PAY
BRACE YOURSELVES
I'M ON MY WAY

'It's him!' Ivy sobbed. 'It's the demon – it has to be. If that is Harriet, maybe he's the one making her forget everything while she's a wolf.'

'Yeah,' Maggie agreed. 'He might be giving us a taste of what's to come. Friends turned into wolves and then turned against us.'

The wolf's growling now became almost a roar that turned into one final *ARROOOOOOOOOOOOOOOOOOOOO!!*

'I think, in this situation,' Ivy said, breathless with fear, 'the best thing we can do is . . .'

'*RUN!*'

The four of them turned on their heels and legged it as fast as humanly (or in Spencer and Eddie's case, vampirically) possible.

The sound of the metal chain rattling rang out into the night as the werewolf threw itself against the gates as hard as it could. Suddenly there was a loud *PING!* as the enormous padlock broke and clattered to the ground. Then a *CRASH!* as the gates exploded open. Finally, the sound of four paws pounding the pavement made Maggie, Ivy, Eddie and Spencer scream as they raced back towards Hokum House.

They needed the witches' help – and they needed it fast.

14
Harriet Has a Rough Night

'HELP! HELP US!' Spencer and Eddie hollered.

'AMETHYST! EMERALD!' yelled Ivy.

'DOUBLE TROUBLE! WE NEED YOU!' Maggie screamed.

They ran up the path and banged on the door to try and wake as many people in the house as possible, but a menacing growl behind them forced them all to turn and face their potential doom.

The creature was quick and had caught up to them with ease. It was crouching low to the ground, ready to pounce. The monster pulled back its lips in a snarl and bared its teeth.

Each tooth was about as large as a child's thumb and looked sharper than any knife in the Hokum House kitchen. The moonlight glinted off the werewolf's fangs, and the children shuddered to imagine what sort of damage teeth like those could do.

'Please don't eat us!' Spencer said desperately.

'Please don't bite us and turn us into a mangy, slobbering monster!' Maggie sobbed.

Suddenly the door to Hokum House opened, and all four of them fell through the doorway and looked up into the unimpressed face of Amethyst.

'Where have you been?!'

'There isn't time to talk, Amethyst! LOOK!' Ivy screeched, jabbing her finger at the sky. The words were still blood red and seemed to have followed them home, twisting to be read the right way up, no matter where you stood.

'Oh . . . oh my goodness.' Amethyst could barely speak, the words catching in her throat.

'That's not the only issue we have.' Maggie pointed back at the darkness outside. The enormous werewolf was easy to miss at first, its fur blending into the shadows of the night.

As soon as Amethyst caught sight of it, she threw up her arms. A purple spell zapped outwards and spread into a shield round the house. The werewolf snarled and jumped back.

'Is . . . is that Harriet?' Amethyst's breath was quick and ragged.

'We don't know, but we think it might be!' Ivy squealed, jumping to her feet and hiding behind the witch.

'Even if it's not Harriet,' said Spencer, 'as a vampire, I can smell the difference between a regular, big dog and a werewolf.'

'And that is definitely a werewolf,' Eddie confirmed, sniffing the air and grimacing.

'Oh my goodness!' Emerald gasped, skittering to the front door from the kitchen.

There was the squeak of chairs and a growing mumbling and muttering as the rest of the Double Trouble Society heard the commotion and came running.

'We think this unfortunate creature might be Harriet Harper,' Amethyst whispered.

'Harriet Harper? The girl with the big hair? And the spiky jacket that doesn't allow anyone within a metre of her?' Emerald clutched a hand to her chest.

Eddie nodded gravely. 'One and the same.'

'No!' Emerald looked horrified. 'But how?'

'No wonder you sensed darkness in this town. We have a clan of vampires and a pack of werewolves right on our doorstep!' said Ivy.

'I don't want to interrupt, but –' Maggie pointed grimly at the wolf – 'we have a time-sensitive situation here and a friend that clearly needs our help.'

'Yes. Sorry. Of course,' said Amethyst, shaking away the thoughts of how and why and focusing on the task at hand.

'How are we gonna get it to calm down so we can figure out if it actually is Harriet?' Spencer asked.

'Oh, that's easy.' Emerald interlinked her fingers and pushed them back so they gave out a gnarly click. 'Ready, sister?'

'Yes, but please be gentle.' Amethyst concentrated all her thoughts on the purple shield that encased the house.

'Always.' Emerald raised her hands, ready to cast her own spell. 'NOW!' she cried.

Amethyst dropped her hands, the protective shield disappeared and, at exactly the same moment, Emerald threw out a bolt of magic. It zapped from her hands like lightning and hit the werewolf right between the eyes. The creature had absolutely no chance of getting out of the way. Emerald's magic had set its course and was never going to miss. The accuracy was astounding.

The wolf let out a small yelp, and then its huge body slumped to the ground. When it hit the path, a huge cloud of fog arose from the spot. The Double Trouble Society ran over. When the fog slowly cleared, Harriet lay sprawled on the ground, her black hair wilder and more unruly than ever. Her mouth hung open, and her tongue lolled out to the side, much like Maggie's dog Frankenstein's did when he was dreaming of chasing rabbits.

'Wow,' said Ivy breathlessly, 'Harriet is gonna have one giant headache when she wakes up . . .'

15

Harriet Can't Remember

Safely back inside Hokum House, Harriet opened her eyes and looked up into the faces of the entire Double Trouble Society.

'Oh no,' she whimpered and sat bolt upright. Then she wobbled slightly and squeezed her eyes shut, touching the point in between her eyes where Emerald's bolt of magic had hit her.

'Oh no indeed,' Amethyst echoed.

'I . . . what did . . . I didn't hurt anyone, did I?' Harriet asked frantically, her eyes scanning everyone's arms and legs and hoping none of them were missing.

'You almost did. But everyone's safe and sound.'

'Why didn't you tell us?' Maggie put her arm round Harriet. At Maggie's kind gesture, Harriet dropped her head into her hands and began to sob.

'I've lost so many friends.' She sniffed, lifting the sleeve of her baggy T-shirt to wipe her nose. 'My parents don't let me stay at anyone else's house, even when it isn't a full moon, just in case I turn in the night. And it's absolutely against the rules to invite someone home. I mean . . . can you imagine? Inviting a human into a den of werewolves.'

Emerald nodded. 'Yes, I can see how that might be slightly problematic.'

'Why? You don't eat humans, do you?' Maggie said, backing away slightly.

'No, no! Not at all! But when a werewolf does turn from human to wolf, you don't want to be standing too close. Claws and teeth tend to fly everywhere.'

'Hang on a minute. You asked if you'd hurt anyone,' said Ivy suddenly. 'Does that mean you can't remember anything about your time as a wolf when you turn back into a human?'

Harriet shook her head sadly. 'Usually, I do remember bits and pieces. I can hang on to a small part of my own mind and personality, but since moving to Crowood Peak –' she hung her head and stared down at her lap, fiddling with her fingers – 'I can't seem to hold on to it tight enough. I disappear entirely, and the wolf takes over.'

She looked up at Amethyst and Emerald, who exchanged wide-eyed glances.

'It scares me a little . . . OK, it terrifies me a whole lot. Because what happens if I forget Harriet the human entirely, and I never turn back? What if I remain a wolf forever? I'd hate that. The fleas are a nightmare, and I can't bear killing rabbits.'

'We won't let that happen, will we?' Maggie said defiantly.

'No, we won't. We never leave a member of the Double Trouble Society behind.' Ivy nodded firmly in agreement.

'You mean . . . I can be part of the gang?' Harriet's eyes lit up and began to well with tears again.

Every member of the Double Trouble Society gave her an enthusiastic thumbs up and clambered into a big group hug with Harriet at the centre.

Ivy found Maggie's elbow and gave it a squeeze, then nodded over at Spencer, who was lurking in the living-room doorway. Eddie was standing next to him and she also caught his eye. He gave her an approving smile, his red eyes glowing.

'You too, Spencer!' Maggie shouted.

'Wait . . . really? But I was so mean to you all!'

'We'll chalk it up to the fact that you were literally turning into a vampire and you haven't slept in about eleven years.'

'Congratulations, Harriet. Congratulations, Spencer.' Amethyst smiled at them.

'Well, it's wonderful to see this group expanding in ways we never expected,' Emerald added with a wry smile.

'Wait,' Ivy said, beginning to pace from one side of the room to the other. 'Spencer came into his vampire powers as soon as he moved here. Harriet can't hold on to her human memories when she's a wolf since coming to live in Crowood Peak . . . Doesn't that seem a bit odd to you?'

Amethyst nodded. 'Yes, it certainly sounds as if there's something strange happening in this town.'

'Whatever it is, it doesn't seem to be lessening our powers. My magic is as strong as ever.' Emerald rubbed her hands together, feeling the magic vibrating beneath her skin.

'Yes, mine too,' said Amethyst, wiggling her fingers and feeling the same pull of power.

'But why does the demon want to increase our powers? Is he getting ready for a fight? A stand-off?' Eddie asked.

Amethyst glanced out of the window where the words in the sky had become a gruesome red haze hanging over the house.

'It certainly seems that way,' she muttered, feeling her magic prickle at the thought.

'Eddie's right,' said Ivy, giving him a nod. 'All these creatures – vampires and werewolves . . . Spencer's family, Harriet's family – they didn't live here before this summer. They must have been called here by something.'

'But by what?' Maggie asked. 'The demon?'

'It wasn't a demon. It was an estate agent,' Harriet said. There was silence as everyone simply stared at her.

'Excuse me?' said Amethyst.

'An estate agent. Y'know . . . someone that helps people buy and sell property.' Harriet shrugged.

'Yes, we all know what an estate agent is. I'm just wondering what on earth you mean?' said Amethyst with a chuckle.

'Well, I don't think we ever had plans to move until one day this woman showed up at our old house. She said she was an estate agent and had found the perfect place for my dad. He let her in, and I thought it was a bit weird, but . . . she said all the right things, and the price was reasonable. I don't ever remember him talking about moving until she showed up, but she made it sound like it was too good a chance to miss.'

'Hang on a second . . .' Spencer said, scratching his head and frowning. 'Did she have red hair? And a bright red suit with a –'

'White belt!' they both said together.

'And white shoes!' Spencer gasped. 'She came to my house too! I saw her talking to my mum in the kitchen one day, then all of a sudden our house was sold and we were moving to Crowood Peak. Same as Harriet, I never heard my parents talking about moving until she turned up on our doorstep.'

Amethyst and Emerald exchanged frightened looks. Amethyst was shaking so much that she had to hold on to the back of the armchair in order to keep upright.

'Harriet. Spencer. I know this might be difficult to remember, but I need you to think very hard. Do you remember what colour eyes this woman, this estate agent, had?'

Harriet and Spencer didn't skip a beat. 'Black,' they chorused.

'I've dreamed of those eyes ever since I saw them,' Harriet whispered, staring into the distance.

'Gave me nightmares for weeks,' added Spencer with a shudder.

'Oh God!' Emerald collapsed to the floor with a squeal. 'He's coming for me! He's coming to get me because the curse was broken!'

'Who?!' Jennifer cried.

'Who's coming?' Jamie asked, running to Emerald's side, but she waved him away, as if coming close to her might put him in danger.

'*What is going on?*' Jemima stamped her foot amid the chaos of Emerald's outburst, creating a little order in the room as everyone fell silent. She turned to Maggie. 'You and Ivy kept us out of your little jaunt to capture a werewolf, and now there's someone with black eyes after Emerald. We're a society, aren't we? Last year we defeated maybe the scariest thing I've ever seen.'

'Maybe?!' Maggie scoffed.

'I watch a lot of scary movies,' said Jemima, shrugging.

'You need to explain to us *exactly* what's going on. Whatever it is, we can handle it – together.'

'Oh, my girl,' Emerald said, clambering to her still wobbly feet. 'If you think that curse was bad, wait until you meet the demon that cast it. Harriet and Spencer only caught a glimpse of it and were haunted for weeks.'

'But they said it was a woman. And you said the demon that cursed the original Crowood Witch was a man.'

'Demons aren't human. They are masters of disguise and trickery. One quick snap of the fingers and it'll have you seeing a house made of sweets and candyfloss. Then, before you know it, you've got a mouth full of bricks and mortar because you tried to take a bite out of the side of an actual house and you've broken all your teeth! It could make you believe you're headed towards a solid road when really it's leading you to the edge of a cliff. And this demon is the worst of the worst.'

'Why would he be after you?' Isaac asked.

'The curse he cast on the original Crowood Witch was his masterpiece. And we smashed it to smithereens. He will not be happy. I expect he's hell-bent on revenge,' said Emerald. 'And, if he's already sent vampires and werewolves to this town, it seems like he's trying to build an army.'

'An army? But we wouldn't turn against you, would we, Harriet?' Spencer stood taller with his chest puffed out as if he was already preparing to fight.

'You might not have any choice in the matter. As Harriet has already proven, when she's in her wolf form, she loses who she really is. If the demon waits until the next full moon when Harriet has no choice but to turn into a wolf, she may not know she's coming after us until it's too late.'

Harriet had begun to tremble at Emerald's words, and then tears slowly started to slip down her cheeks.

'I don't want to be this monster any more,' she sobbed. 'It's the reason I have no friends. I just want to be a normal kid.'

'Harriet, you are way better than a normal kid!' Maggie rushed over to her, her frustration getting the better of her. 'You have superpowers! It's AMAZING! Normal kids dream of being what you are. Don't wish that away!'

'That's right, Harriet.' Ivy rubbed her shoulders. 'And we won't let that horrible demon make you do anything you don't want to do.'

'How?' Harriet sniffled.

'Yes, Ivy. How?' said Amethyst, crossing her arms.

'I don't know yet, but we'll figure it out. Because that's what friends do,' Ivy said with a firm nod.

'Because that's what the Double Trouble Society does,' echoed Maggie.

'Right. So we need a plan.' Amethyst sighed heavily. 'What do we know so far? Ivy, make a list.'

Ivy grabbed her notebook from the coffee table and began to scrawl on a new page.

'We know the demon is moving creatures like vampires and werewolves, and potentially some others we don't know about, to Crowood Peak,' said Emerald.

'Probably to build an army against us,' Amethyst added.

'But if we're clever we could get Spencer's and Harriet's families on our side before the demon makes his move,' Eddie suggested.

'Are you thinking what I'm thinking, sister?' Emerald asked, and Amethyst nodded.

'What is it?' Maggie and Ivy said together.

'It's a very old and very powerful piece of magic,' said Amethyst. 'It's time to call . . . a town meeting.'

16
Orville Takes a Picture

The blood-red words had vanished from the sky by morning, and a town meeting was called for that weekend. Amethyst and Emerald were certain the demon would wait until the next full moon to ensure that the werewolves would all be susceptible to his dark magic, making them forget who they were as humans and forcing them to do his bidding. Luckily, it was also when Amethyst's magic would be at its strongest. The demon would know that, however, and might have a trick up his sleeve to counteract her magic, so they had to be ready for anything.

The witches and the Double Trouble Society therefore

had just under a month to get ready for whatever the demon was about to throw at them. If they were to get all the vampires and werewolves on their side, they needed to make them feel welcome and accepted in Crowood Peak among the humans. They had to prove to them that this was a place where they wouldn't have to hide their true identities, a feat that didn't seem too difficult considering the citizens of Crowood had already welcomed two witches (one of whom had attempted to turn all the adults to stone) with (mostly) open arms. A few fangs and claws probably weren't going to scare the majority of humans living in the town.

Until the meeting, the Double Trouble Society were to return to school. Amethyst and Emerald refused to cast a spell on their teachers to make them forget that they'd left school early the previous day.

'You need to learn to live life without the use of magic,' Amethyst explained. 'You can't always rely on me and Emerald to get you out of trouble whenever you need it. Even though you left school to help Eddie, you still have to realize that there are consequences to your actions. We won't always be able to wave a magic wand and make things better for you.'

'Besides,' said Emerald, laughing, 'detention is nothing compared to the dark curse you defeated last year.' Then her laughter faded. 'And will be nothing compared to what that demon might have in store for us all.'

★

Ivy had never had detention before and, as the end of the school day and detention drew nearer, she got more and more nervous.

'Ivy, why are you so scared?' Maggie asked, pulling on her backpack at the end of the last lesson.

Maggie had had several detentions, mainly for talking too much or not handing in her homework, and once for mixing the wrong chemicals in science and causing a minor but very loud explosion in the lab.

'They just make you sit there in silence and read or get on with homework.'

'Sometimes they make you write lines if you've done something particularly bad,' said Eddie, trailing behind them.

Eddie's parents had been told that he had contracted a rare but mild illness that turned his eyes red and gave him insomnia (insomnia is the name for when you can't sleep very well, and you lie awake and toss and turn all night). Given that he could still eat normal food, he would still be able to join in family dinners. The Double Trouble Society just had to help him sneak out every few nights after dark so he could hunt.

It all seemed to be falling into place, even if it was falling into a place none of them had anticipated. Eddie and Spencer had formed a new brotherly bond that meant they helped each other learn how to be proper vampires. Eddie seemed to be fine around humans when he had fed, but he kept a respectful distance just in case. He was still getting to grips with all the new smells and sounds that came with his heightened senses, and he also didn't want to make anyone in the society feel uncomfortable by being too close.

Eddie sometimes caught Ivy staring at him with a sad look in her eyes, so every once in a while he'd catch up with his friends and throw a few pop-quiz questions Ivy's way, just like old times.

'Oh,' said Ivy. 'Well, detention doesn't sound too bad. Maybe I'll just get a head start on all my homework then. Or maybe I'll use the time to finish the book I'm reading. Or maybe I could write a quiz for Darla.'

'Only Ivy Eerie could find a way to enjoy detention,' said Jemima, joining their group as she came out of another classroom.

'Are we all here?' Maggie asked as they gathered outside the door to the detention room. She did a headcount. Eddie, Isaac, Spencer, Jennifer, Jamie, Jemima, Harriet, Ivy and herself were all present. 'Here we go then, Ivy. Welcome to detention.'

Maggie opened the door, expecting the Double Trouble Society to be the only people in detention that day, but found someone already sitting there, waiting for a teacher to arrive.

'Orville? What are you in for?' Maggie asked, putting her bag down on her usual desk.

'I lost track of time and accidentally missed maths. I was taking pictures down by the pond near the playground.'

'Awesome.' Isaac grinned. 'Find anything good?'

Orville shrugged. 'Some tadpoles have started to grow legs. They were pretty cool.'

'You know they're called froglets?' Isaac informed him.

'Whatever happened to that thing that was following you, Orville?' Harriet asked.

'Did you ever figure out what it was?' Maggie opened her bag and pulled out the book she'd been reading, *Galactic Musicians*.

'It's still following me,' said Orville huffily, doodling on his notepad. 'And I'm sure it keeps taking pencils out of my pencil case. They always end up spilled all over the bottom of my satchel. Loads get broken. My mum can't understand why I'm always asking her to buy me new ones. She keeps threatening to take my camera away from me. "If you can't be trusted with a few pencils –" ' he mimicked his mother in a high-pitched, squeaky voice – ' "how can you be trusted with a beautiful camera like that!" '

'Are you sure you're not just forgetting to zip up the pencil case before you pack it away?' Ivy asked gently, but Orville instantly knitted his eyebrows together in annoyance.

'Why is it so easy for you to believe in witches, but you can't believe that there's something following me?'

'We have proof that Emerald and Amethyst are witches. We don't have proof that there's something following you,'

Ivy said, choosing the desk next to Maggie and taking out her beloved notebook and a fluffy pink pen.

'No, he's right, Ivy,' said Maggie. 'We believed that Amethyst was a witch long before we had hard evidence.' Then she dropped her voice to a whisper and said to Ivy, 'And, more recently, we've believed lots of other things that we didn't have proof of.' She turned back to Orville. 'Sometimes it's just a gut feeling. Intuition, right?'

'Yeah. That's exactly what it is. I *know* something's following me. I've felt it since the day I came to Crowood Peak, and I've not been able to shake that feeling.'

'Since you came to Crowood?' Harriet asked, a little breathless. The gang all looked at one another.

'Sorry, Orville.' Ivy shook her head. 'Maggie's totally right. Is there anything we can do?'

'I wish there was, but how can you catch something you can't see?' Orville hung his head sadly and carried on doodling.

Maggie chuckled. 'That sounds like a challenge if ever I heard one.'

'Yes, and now I know how I'm going to spend my detention! Trying to figure out how to catch something invisible!' Ivy hurriedly began to flip to a fresh clean page in her notebook.

'Thanks! Hey, before the teacher gets here, how about a photo?' Orville jiggled the camera that hung round his neck. 'It'd be cool to get one of the gang altogether.'

'I don't think we've ever had our picture taken before. Not all of us,' said Maggie.

'But we can't! Darla isn't here,' said Jennifer.

'I can take another photograph when she is around,' Orville assured her. 'I need to practise, anyway. I want to be a photographer for a big magazine or a newspaper when I'm older. I'm hoping to do it for the school paper here at Crowood.' He began tinkering around with his film camera.

'See, I told you I was right to be worried about where he'd put that photo of me that he took on the first day,' Spencer muttered to Ivy and Maggie.

'OK, ready? Everyone budge up now.' The gang shuffled together at the side of the classroom, with their backs to the school windows that looked on to the playing field. Orville waved his hands about to get everyone closer together or a bit to the left or a bit to the right. 'That's perfect! OK, everyone, say . . .'

'GHOST!' shouted Jemima as Orville snapped the photo.

'I was going to say cheese, but sure, you can all say whatever you want! Let's take another one because you weren't smiling, Jemima.'

'NO! I MEAN . . . THERE'S A GHOST! THERE! SITTING AT ORVILLE'S DESK!' Jemima pointed with a shaking finger to where he'd just been sitting. His pen was standing up on its own and wiggling about in the air, scrawling on the page of his exercise book where he'd been doodling.

'No way!' whispered Maggie.

'OK, stay calm, everyone,' said Ivy, backing away from the moving pen and grabbing her notebook. 'I have a list of facts all about ghosts.'

Spencer laughed. 'Of course you do.'

'Why don't you seem as freaked out as the rest of us?' Jennifer was trembling, unable to move from where she was sitting, fear rooting her firmly to the spot.

Spencer simply pointed to himself and said, 'Vampire. Duh.'

She nodded. 'Fair point.'

Then Jennifer, Jamie, Jemima and Isaac all shot behind Spencer and Eddie and felt a little safer for it.

'What does your list say, Ivy?'

'There are lots of different types of ghosts. Some ghosts are simply echoes of the people they used to be, repeating the things they once did when they were alive over and over and over again. Sort of stuck in a loop. Some ghosts are the souls of people who died suddenly or unexpectedly and have unfinished business, unable to move on until they . . . well . . . finish that business. And other ghosts are called poltergeists. They're angry ghosts who can move things . . . around . . .' Ivy trailed off as she looked up slowly at the pen moving of its own accord across Orville's exercise book.

'OK . . . so we know this is a poltergeist then.' Maggie gulped.

'Didn't you just say they're angry ghosts?' said Orville.

Ivy nodded. 'Yes. Usually, they're able to move things because their anger is so potent it transcends their spirit form and echoes through into the real world.'

'But that doesn't mean this ghost is angry with us. It just means the ghost has something to be upset about and is trying to find a way to solve that problem,' Eddie said calmly.

'So how do we find out what it wants?' Orville shuddered, his camera rattling against the buttons of his tweed jacket.

'I reckon reading whatever it's writing might be a good start.' Maggie gestured to the exercise book.

'Good idea,' Orville said, but stayed exactly where he was. 'Well, don't look at me! I'm not going near it! I'm the one it's been following around for ages. Clearly, it's angry at *me*.'

'All right, don't get your pants in a twist,' said Jemima. She puffed out her chest and declared, 'I'll do it.'

'Be careful, Jemima,' Ivy warned as Jemima took one careful step towards Orville's desk and the scribbling pen.

As she got closer, the writing became more rapid, the pen darting this way and that on the page, making scratching noises as it went. She took another step, and suddenly the pen stopped writing and rose in the air, the nib pointing directly at Jemima, almost as if it was *looking* at her. Jemima, braver than anyone, took one last step towards the desk.

The pen flew at her. With the precision of a dart and the speed of an arrow, it whooshed through the air. Luckily, Jemima managed to duck just in time. The pen swerved, did a loop round the edge of the classroom and then returned to Orville's desk. It flew directly up into the air and then dive-bombed as quickly and as hard as it could and pierced the wood of Orville's desk with a *THWUMP!* and then a *DOING!* Now it was sticking out of the table like a knife in a butcher's block.

Jemima picked herself up off the ground and dusted herself down, panting heavily from the excitement of it all.

'That's definitely one angry ghost,' whispered Maggie.

'What does the note say?' Ivy asked Jemima, still unwilling to get close to the pen in case it started attacking again.

Jemima had no such qualms now that the danger was less imminent. She strode up to the desk, grabbed Orville's exercise book and looked. The writing was messy and frantic.

'It's hard to make out. Lots of the words are overlapping. But it says . . . "*Run, Orville! Run!*" '

'That's all?'

'Yes, but –' Jemima turned the exercise book round to show the rest of the group – 'it says it over and over and over again.'

'OHMYGOD!' Orville shrieked, clapping his hands on to his head.

'OK, let's not panic,' Ivy said quickly, running over to

grab the exercise book and rip out the page. 'Not until we've shown this to Amethyst and Emerald.'

'Don't panic? DON'T PANIC?!' Orville was panting heavily. 'That's easy for you to say! You don't have an angry poltergeist sending messages from beyond the grave telling you to run!'

'But run from what?' Isaac asked.

'Run from the ghost itself?' Jamie suggested.

'Run from danger?' Harriet's voice was still wobbly from worry. Even though she was a werewolf and probably less susceptible to whatever a ghost might have to offer, she couldn't muster the same courage as Eddie and Spencer.

'We can't know for sure until we do some proper investigating,' said Ivy.

'Yes, and first things first . . . we need to get that photo developed immediately,' added Maggie.

'Eh?' Orville clutched his camera protectively.

'You took a photo of us all just before Jemima spotted the ghost, right?' said Ivy.

'Do you really think something might show up?'

'It might just be an orb of light or something, but at least that could be some sort of proof that it was a ghost and not someone playing a prank on us.'

'There's no way that was a prank!' Orville's voice was getting increasingly shrill.

'I know, but when we explain this to Amethyst and Emerald we need something to show them. Proof. Evidence. Something that doesn't make it sound like we were just seeing things or one of the older kids in the school was trying to spook us,' Ivy explained, carefully putting the torn-out page from Orville's exercise book in the back of her notebook to keep it flat as she packed it in her school bag.

'Ivy's right. For a pair of witches, they do need an awful lot of proof of something before they believe us,' said Maggie with a sigh.

'Adults. They can never just . . . believe, can they?' Jemima rolled her eyes.

'Ready?' Ivy asked the group, but they all looked at her blankly.

'Wait . . . what?' Maggie laughed nervously. 'Ivy, we can't just skip detention.'

'Why not?' Ivy shrugged.

'This is a very different side to you . . . I like it. But what's got into you?'

'I guess I've just learned that sometimes you need to bend the rules a little when something bigger is at stake. And currently what's at stake is the safety of this town and everyone who lives here. I personally think that's worth the risk.'

Maggie grinned. 'All in favour of skipping detention for the greater good, say aye!'

'Aye!' They all raised their hands without a second thought.

'Right, let's get out of here before the teacher on detention duty arrives. *Go! Go! Go!*'

And together they raced out of detention and into Orville's domain . . . the dark room.

17
The Boy in the Photo

For the rest of the students, school was done for the day, but for the Double Trouble Society things were just getting started. They crept along the corridor on tiptoe, dodging the teachers until they finally reached the door marked DARK ROOM.

'When we get inside, please be careful. I'm not meant to be in here without a teacher's supervision. *Don't. Touch. Anything*,' Orville instructed as he opened the door. It was a small room, so they had to squash and squeeze themselves in until they could barely move.

'Stop shoving me!' hissed Jemima.

'Get your elbow out of my face then!' growled Jamie.

'Ouch, my hair's caught in the zip of your bag!' Jennifer squeaked.

'I don't really like small dark spaces,' said Isaac, who spent most of his time in natural, wide, open-air spaces like parks and ponds.

'OK, OK, the only way this is gonna pan out is if we all pull together,' said Maggie. 'Orville needs to work in this space, and we need to hide from the teachers to make sure they don't find us. So follow his lead. What can we do to help, Orville?'

'It looks like someone else has been in here developing photos. They might be back soon, as they're only halfway through the process. So let's just quickly develop our photograph and get out of here.'

Orville got to work. There were chemicals and canisters, a machine that enlarged photos from tiny negatives on a reel of film and baths that photographs had to sit in for thirty seconds. The others pushed and shoved and shuffled round the room when Orville needed to move until finally he laid an A4 sheet of photo paper into its final bath. They all crowded round to watch the photograph appear.

'Hey, look, there we are! I can see our faces!'

'Well . . . most of our faces, anyway,' Eddie said, nudging Spencer and indicating the empty spaces in the group where they'd been standing when Orville took the photo.

'What do you mean?' Orville asked.

Eddie pointed to the photograph again. He and Eddie were nowhere to be seen. In fact, you could see Ivy and Jamie's arms held out at their sides like they were perched on the shoulders of two invisible men.

'Did you two duck out of the way for a laugh?' Orville chuckled, but it was breathy and unconvincing. Eddie and Spencer remained silent and turned their heads to Ivy and Maggie. Ivy sighed.

'Orville might as well know, seeing as he's helping us now, but you need to swear you won't tell another soul. A "cross your heart and hope to die and stick a needle in your eye" sort of promise,' Ivy said in a threatening tone.

Orville crossed his heart quickly and mimed poking himself in the eye. Ivy nodded at Eddie and Spencer.

'We're vampires,' Eddie said calmly.

'No, you're not,' Orville said blankly.

'Yes, we are.' Spencer concentrated for a moment and thought of all the heartbeats in the room and all the blood coursing through everyone's veins just long enough for his canine teeth to elongate and come to a very sharp point. When Spencer shook himself out of it and opened his eyes, Orville had tried to edge so far away from both of them that he was squashing Harriet.

'OK . . . so you are.' He whimpered.

'This is SO COOL!' Spencer laughed, grabbing the

photo from Orville with one hand and punching the air with his other fist, accidentally disturbing a string of photographs hanging up to dry above them. 'Whoops! It's just that I've waited so long to *not* see my reflection or my photograph. You don't know how many selfies I've taken over the years in the hopes that I didn't appear. This is the first time I've ever had the pleasure of not seeing myself. It's awesome.'

'Do you know what isn't awesome, though? HIM!' Orville pointed with a shaking finger, and together the group gasped.

'No way!' Maggie yelped.

They all gawped and rubbed their eyes in complete disbelief at what they were seeing. In the photograph, Orville's pen wasn't floating in mid-air. It was being held by a boy about the same age as Orville, maybe ten or eleven, and he was looking directly at the camera, but his eyes were white lights in their sockets. He was wearing old-fashioned clothes: little blue shorts with a puffy white shirt, blue braces and a blue neckerchief to match.

'OK . . . so we've proved that Orville definitely isn't going mad. He absolutely is being haunted by a ghost,' Ivy said, a little spooked by the creepy image.

'I wonder who it is?' Jennifer asked. 'He doesn't look angry, just . . . sad. And scared.'

'Why was he telling Orville to run?' Jamie said.

'I don't think we'll figure out what this ghost wants unless we talk to him,' Ivy decided.

'Talk to him?' Maggie scoffed. 'He's a ghost! How are we going to manage that?!'

'Well, he found a way to talk to us, didn't he?' Ivy said, tapping her school bag with the note tucked neatly inside. 'And, besides, I bet Amethyst and Emerald have a spell or a potion or something that will make him appear to us so we can have a proper conversation. Now that we have proof that there is a ghost following Orville, they *have* to listen to us.'

Amethyst and Emerald did indeed listen, and listen intently. They carefully examined the photographic evidence of the boy haunting Orville. Then they shared a look of despair.

'So not only is this demon calling all manner of creatures to arms, he's woken the dead to join his witch-hunt!' Emerald cried, throwing up her hands.

'Yes, it does concern me that other ghosts may have arisen too. However, this ghost has managed to send a message, and you're absolutely right, Ivy.' Amethyst put her hands together as if in prayer and then pressed her fingers to her lips, deep in thought.

'I am?' Ivy asked.

'Why are you surprised? You're always right.' Eddie nudged her, and she couldn't help but smile.

'Yes, Ivy. We need to find a way to have a conversation with this little lad. He might know something that could help us fight the demon when he decides to strike.'

'And if that happens to be the next full moon, we don't have a huge amount of time.'

'But how do we contact someone from beyond the grave?' Isaac asked.

'A seance, of course,' said Amethyst, as if it was the most obvious thing in the world.

'A . . . a . . . seance?' Harriet trembled. 'I've only ever seen them in movies, and they always end badly. Someone gets possessed, or a ghost attaches itself to someone, follows them home and then haunts them for the rest of their lives.' Her voice suddenly became very high-pitched.

'Well, this ghost is already attached to me, so I doubt he's gonna want to follow anyone else home,' Orville said. 'Besides, I think he's stuck in the school. I only ever feel him following me when I'm there, never when I'm in my own house. Otherwise I don't think I would have slept the whole time I've lived in Crowood Peak.' He shuddered.

'Oh, that does make things tricky,' Amethyst tutted. 'We'll have to carry out the seance at school if the ghost is stuck there.'

'The school would never allow that. Your headmistress barely lets us anywhere near the place,' said Emerald sulkily.

'I thought everyone loved you two,' said Maggie.

Amethyst shook her head. 'The majority of the town opened its arms to us after the blue moon last year, but . . . not everyone was as forthcoming with their acceptance.'

'And annoyingly one of those people is your new headmistress,' said Emerald grimly.

'Mrs Stern's the worst. She told me that, even though I'm top of the school, I'll never make any friends beyond Crowood School because no one likes a know-it-all.' Ivy lowered her eyes.

'I got the opposite.' Maggie chuckled. 'She told me it was a good job I'm friendly as I'll always have to rely on other people to get ahead in life because I'm not very clever!'

Amethyst gave a sharp intake of breath at that.

'She told me to crochet myself a pair of wings and buzz off. I was just saying good morning!' Jennifer added.

'She's forever telling me to wash the mud off my hands, but –' Isaac showed them his palms, as filthy as ever – 'I think that's fair.'

'She never even speaks to me,' said Jemima. 'Just automatically gives me detention if she catches sight of me. Once I asked her why she does that, and she said it's because I'm *always* up to no good, and if I'm not up to no good now I will be eventually, and it's better to get ahead of the problem.' Jemima crossed her arms. 'I'm not *that* much of a troublemaker!'

The whole gang turned to her with a collective look that said *yeah, right*.

'Well, I'm not that much of a troublemaker *any more*.'

'OK, so we definitely won't get the approval of Mrs Stern. That means we'll just have to be a little sneaky, which apparently comes second nature to you lot now.'

'We don't know what you're talking about . . .' Maggie clasped her hands behind her back and smiled sweetly.

'Oh really? Tell me, Ivy, how was detention?' Amethyst asked, looking Ivy directly in the eye. Ivy felt herself grow hotter and redder, a bead of sweat trickling down between her shoulder blades.

'OK, OK! We didn't go! We needed to develop this photo because I knew – I just *knew* – we'd find something!' Ivy jumped up and down. 'And I was right! We did! We did find something really important!'

'And we figured the safety of the town was more important than our punishment. We can do detention another time when we know Crowood isn't going to come to any harm,' added Maggie.

Amethyst paused before she replied, realizing that the children were, in fact, right.

'When this is over, you're all going to have a week's detention. Even if the school won't let you serve it there, I will make sure you come back here after school and sit and do homework for an hour. No chatting, no telly, no nothing. You hear me?'

'Yes, Amethyst! Of course, Amethyst!' Everyone nodded, although they secretly hoped that it might be forgotten once all this was over.

'All right.' Emerald rubbed her hands together, creating little sparks of green magic. 'There's only one thing for it. Tonight we're breaking into Crowood School and holding a seance.'

18
Holding a Seance

Sneaking into school when it was closed wasn't a particularly difficult feat when you had witches on your side. There was no door or gate they couldn't unlock, no window they couldn't open, and no one had to worry about being seen because Amethyst cast an invisibility spell over the group before they left. As long as they stuck together within her little purple bubble, they'd be fine.

After dark, they had all snuck out of their houses and met at Hokum House so together they could make their way down the road and over the hill to school. Amethyst clicked her fingers, and the huge padlock that connected two ends of a very large chunky chain simply opened on its own and clattered to the ground. Once they were safely through the gates, Amethyst put the chain and lock back.

'Don't want anyone following us,' she whispered.

The school corridors were eerie at night-time. The absence of children's chatter and laughter made the whole place feel cavernous. Every single one of their footsteps sounded like a klaxon, giving away their whereabouts. By the time they reached the school hall where assemblies were usually held, they were all walking on tiptoe and holding their breath. None of them had realized that at some point along the way they'd all reached out to each other and were holding hands, arms, hems of coats, anything they could grab in order to feel like a united front.

'Right,' Amethyst said, but even in a whisper her voice sounded deafening in the silence. 'I think here will do.'

She nodded at Emerald, who produced a chunky candle and a bell from the deep pockets hidden within her green coat. With a wave of her hand, Amethyst lit the candle and placed it on the floor, putting the bell next to it. 'Everyone sit in a circle round the candle.'

'What's the bell for?' asked Maggie.

'Sometimes ghosts find it hard to communicate with words. Their voices can't quite break through the veil between their world and ours. So you have to give them an alternative. OK, now everyone hold hands. That's it.'

As they all grabbed their friends' fingers, everyone realized their hands had gone as cold as ice. Two of the group no longer had beating hearts to pump warm blood round their bodies, but there wasn't even a sweaty, clammy palm among the humans, despite their nerves and fear of what was about to happen.

'Are we all ready?' Amethyst looked round the circle at the pale, drained faces of the Double Trouble Society. 'The most important thing you need to remember is not to break the circle, OK?' They all nodded. 'Emerald, would you like to do the honours?'

'No, sister.' Emerald's voice was hoarse and croaky, and on either side of her Jemima and Jamie could feel her hands trembling. They squeezed her fingers and held her steady. 'Spirits are your domain. Besides, the moon is out, and your magic is strong. I can barely feel the earth through the concrete of this floor.'

Amethyst cleared her throat. 'If there is a spirit here, we mean you no harm.' It was a shock to hear her voice ring out loud and clear after all their whispering. 'We wish to speak with you, so please, if you are here, make yourself known.'

They all held their breath. But nothing happened. A wave of relief washed over everyone. Amethyst tried again.

'We know there's a spirit in this school tormenting our friend Orville. We would like to find out why. Please speak to us. We want to help you.'

'Look!' whispered Orville, nodding towards the flame of the candle, which had begun to flicker, as if someone was trying to blow it out from across the room.

Each of them focused on the flame, willing whoever it was to give them more of a sign, to send a clearer message that they were there, when all of a sudden the flame was extinguished. There was a collective gasp.

'Don't break the circle! Whatever you do, do not let go of each other's hands,' Emerald said urgently.

'The bell! Look at the bell!' Ivy whimpered. It was beginning to lift off the floor as if someone was picking it up.

'Good! Good! Whoever you are, we will ask you questions. Ring once for yes, twice for no. Do you understand?'

RING!

The group looked at each other in disbelief.

'You're doing so well, spirit. Now, do you know Orville Thomas?'

RING!

'How?' asked Orville.

'You can only ask yes or no questions, doofus,' said Jemima scornfully.

'Was it less than fifty years ago that you shuffled off your mortal coil?' Amethyst helped.

RING! RING!

'No. So more than fifty?' she asked.

RING!

'More than one hundred?'

RING!

'More than two hundred?'

RING!

'Three hundred years ago?'

RING!

'Three hundred years ago . . . that's odd.' Amethyst frowned.

'Could just be a coincidence?' said Emerald hopefully.

'Are you the spirit in the photo these children took earlier today?'

RING!

'So you're about the same age as the children in this circle?'

RING!

'Ivy . . . help me. List the names of the children killed by the Crowood Witch.'

'Clarence Cauldwell, Elijah Brown . . .'

'Is your name Clarence Cauldwell?'

RING! RING!

'Is your name Elijah Brown?'

RING! RING!

'Oh my goodness . . .' Orville took a deep breath. 'I know who it is.'

Everyone looked at him. His face had gone as white as a sheet.

'Is your name Orin Thomas?' he asked.

RING-A-LING-A-LING-A-LING-A-LING-A-LING-A-LING!

'I think that's a yes, Orville.'

'It's my great-great-great-great-great-great-great-great-uncle, Orin Thomas. Why did you tell me to run?' Suddenly the bell clattered to the floor and began to spin round and round and round until it abruptly stopped, its handle pointing at Emerald. They looked at her, but she seemed as clueless as them.

'Me? What have I done?' she yelped.

'Is there really no way we can speak to Orin properly? This yes-or-no thing is really frustrating,' said Maggie.

'Wait, can you hear that?' asked Isaac. 'Ivy, I think it's coming from your bag.'

Ivy's school bag was sitting in front of her and, sure enough, there was a crackling sound coming from inside. Ivy was about to let go of Harriet and Maggie's hands, but Amethyst said, 'Don't break the circle!'

'I've got an idea.' Ivy raised her hands and, without breaking contact, she moved Maggie and Harriet's hands to her shoulders. Now she had her hands free to open her bag and remove her pink walkie-talkie, which was fizzing and crackling. Ivy pressed the channel button over and over, listening intently.

Channels one to twelve were just white noise. Then, as she hit channel thirteen, a boy's voice shouted, 'RUN! RUN! WHY AREN'T YOU RUNNING! IT'S HER! IT'S THE CROWOOD WITCH!'

'Hello? Hello? Is that Orin?' Ivy spoke into the walkie-talkie.

'YES! RUN! SHE'S GOING TO EAT YOUR HEART!' the boy cried.

'Orin, calm down! This isn't the Crowood Witch! It's our friend Emerald!' Maggie shouted as Ivy held the button down so they could all be heard.

'That *witch* is no friend to you. She's the one the curse has passed to. She's returned to claim the thirteenth child that she never got her hands on!' Orin had begun to sob on the end of the line.

'That was true a year ago, Orin,' Emerald said sadly. 'But it seems you've missed a lot while your spirit has been at rest.'

'W-what?' Orin sniffed.

'You're right, Orin,' Ivy explained. 'Emerald was the person who inherited the curse, but we destroyed it last year. Now she's just a normal neighbourhood witch. Well, as normal as a witch can be. And she has no taste for the hearts of human children.'

'I promise I don't. I prefer croissants these days,' said Emerald earnestly.

'Oh. Where have I been? Why have I only just woken up?'

'We're not entirely sure yet, Orin, but we think the demon who cast the curse in the first place is coming back to take his revenge. We think he's building an army to take us on. He's brought vampires and werewolves here too.'

'The best of luck to you, my friends,' said Orin. 'The ghosts of the twelve children his curse killed are awake, and there's not a chance we would fight on his side.'

'Really? So would you fight for us if the time came for battle?' Amethyst asked.

'Who is that speaking now?'

'Sorry. I'm Amethyst. Emerald's sister.'

'Two good witches in one town? I wish I'd lived three hundred years later.' Orin chuckled. 'We'll be on your side until the end, won't we?' Orin asked, and suddenly the voices of eleven other children piled on top of each other. A chorus of:

'Absolutely!'

'Of course we will!'

'We're with you, witches!'

'Oh, and Orville?' Orin said.

'Yeah?' Orville replied loud enough for the walkie-talkie to pick up his voice.

'You're making our family really proud.'

'Proud? Why?' asked Orville.

'You are willing to take on the demon that killed me. No other Thomas was brave enough to do that when I was alive.'

There was a moment when the whole Double Trouble Society looked at Orville, and it took him a moment to swallow the lump in his throat before he said, 'Thanks, Uncle Orin.' Then the walkie-talkie returned to static.

'I think it's OK to break the circle now,' said Amethyst.

Everyone let go and stretched out their aching fingers, only now realizing just how tightly they'd been gripping each other's hands.

'Well, that's quite a turn-up for the books, isn't it?' said Amethyst.

'Definitely,' said Emerald quietly.

'When your dads created the Double Trouble Society, I bet they never expected that a bunch of ghosts would one day join the ranks!' Amethyst said with a smile.

Ivy laughed. 'To be honest, I don't think Maggie and I expected that either.'

'Well, Orville, at least the person haunting you turned out to be a guardian angel,' said Maggie.

'I think it's time we got you all home and to bed. Otherwise your parents will wonder why teachers are calling home about you falling asleep in class.' Amethyst rose to her feet and gestured for them all to stand up too.

'But before we go,' said Ivy, 'Maggie and I have something we'd like to say.'

The two girls walked over to Orville. They both held out their hands for him to shake and said, 'Welcome to the Double Trouble Society.'

19
A Town Meeting

Amethyst and Emerald needed to get all the creatures together and explain to them that they'd been tricked into moving to Crowood Peak by a demon who wanted to create a monster army. It wasn't going to be easy.

The Double Trouble Society made eye-catching flyers, using colourful pens, glitter and stickers. They were designed to go through the letterboxes of everyone in town. However, Amethyst helped to enchant them so that anyone with magic running through their veins would receive a flyer that said:

URGENT!
THE WITCHES REQUEST YOUR PRESENCE AT A CROWOOD SCHOOL HALL MEETING.
THEY NEED YOUR HELP!
THIS FRIDAY AT 7 P.M. SHARP.

However, any humans reading the same flyer would see:

CLEANING SERVICE
CALL 0800-MOON-SHINE
WE'LL MAKE YOUR HOUSE SHINE
BRIGHTER THAN THE MOON!

The meeting had to be held in the school hall so that the ghosts could come as well. Maggie and Ivy had plastered flyers all over the school noticeboards in the hope that any ghosts floating around would see them.

At five minutes to seven on Friday, the Double Trouble Society convened in the school hall, but none of them had much to say to each other. There was no excitement. Just fretting and pacing and hoping and praying.

Amethyst and Emerald had written, in giant cursive writing, *WELCOME, ALL!* on a blackboard they'd propped up at the back of the stage. The two witches were standing together at the lectern, poring over their notes and practising how they'd deliver their news.

'Do you think the vampires and werewolves will be OK being in the same room?' asked Maggie curiously.

Harriet, Eddie and Spencer all looked at each other and then at her. 'Good point,' said Harriet, and Maggie laughed.

'I told you. We aren't sworn enemies or anything,' Spencer explained. 'We just don't really run in the same circles.'

'Hey, hey, I think people are starting to arrive!' said Jemima excitedly.

'I told my dad he *had* to come, and he seemed to understand that this was important. He hates demons,' said Spencer.

Jamie shuddered. 'Who doesn't?'

'Explain to me again what the difference is between dark-magic creatures like vampires or werewolves and a demon?' asked Orville.

'Dark magic is selfish magic,' Emerald explained. 'Creatures that use it do so for their own gain. For example, vampires drink blood because they need to eat! It doesn't necessarily make them evil.'

'Demons on the other hand –' Amethyst chipped in, tapping a wad of notecards together on the lectern so they were straight and neat – 'are born evil and happily act on their evil whims and don't care if they hurt people. In fact, they enjoy it.'

'Hello? We're here for the meeting?'

Two men around the age of fifty stepped into the room. Not a single member of the Double Trouble Society had seen either of them before. One of them, the taller one, wore a blue corduroy suit with a well-ironed pink shirt underneath. He had long red hair that he wore in a neat plait that snaked all the way down his back almost to the back of his knees. The other man had on a pink suit, with a blue shirt underneath, and he had hair almost as white-blonde as Amethyst's.

'Yes, please do come in. I'm Amethyst and this is my sister, Emerald.' They all politely shook hands. 'I'm so sorry, but I don't believe we've ever met.'

'No, we moved here last week. I'm Bellamy,' said the man in the blue suit. 'And this is Birch.' He gestured to the man in the pink suit, his chest puffed out with pride and a dopey grin on his face. 'We've mostly kept ourselves to ourselves since we arrived and . . . well, I guess, seeing as you're witches, we can tell you that we put diversion spells on our house to make sure no one ever really saw it. Anyone who happened to look at it would immediately turn away.'

'Spells?' Maggie asked.

'Yes. We're warlocks,' explained Birch.

'You have moon magic,' said Amethyst breathlessly, taking his hand to shake again, their magic greeting each other under the surface of their fingertips. But then she pulled away quickly. 'It's dark magic . . .'

'We're necromancers,' Birch explained. Maggie raised an eyebrow, so he went on. 'We talk to the dead. Raise them from their graves occasionally, if needs be.'

'We're private investigators, you see? We work closely with the police force when there's been a murder. Sometimes it's hard to figure out whodunnit unless you ask the victim yourselves!'

'Wow!' Maggie marvelled. 'That is *so* cool!'

Bellamy and Birch laughed. 'I guess it is kind of cool.'

'Are you kidding? You get to talk to people who are no longer around! And you solve murder cases! What's the most gruesome thing you've ever seen? How did they get killed? Ohmygod, I want to know EVERYTHING.' Maggie was practically bouncing up and down with excitement.

'OK, Maggie, let them sit down,' said Amethyst, giggling. 'You can talk to them after the meeting.'

Next to arrive were Harriet's mother, father, grandmother and her baby brother, Rex. They all had the same raven-black, unkempt hair and eyes as dark and mysterious as outer space.

'It's a pleasure to meet you both.' Harriet's father, Bruce, shook Amethyst's hand with such force that Amethyst wobbled all over. Harriet's grandmother, Linda, went in for a great big hug with both Amethyst and Emerald at the same time, and they smiled at each other over her shoulders.

'A pleasure. Such a pleasure! Harriet's told us all about you.'

'All good, I promise!' Harriet crossed her heart.

More and more people filtered into the town hall. Every now and then, the door would open, but no one would arrive, and all the children gave each other a meaningful glance.

'Are the hinges on that door on the blink?' Bruce laughed.

'It's just . . . um . . . the wind,' said Maggie hurriedly.

'But we're inside . . .' Linda muttered.

'I think it's time everyone took their seats.' Ivy clapped her hands together. 'The meeting is about to begin!' she announced.

'Look how many people there are,' Spencer whispered to the others. They were sitting in front of the little stage on which Amethyst and Emerald now stood.

'These are all magical and mythical creatures!' Jemima said. 'How? How can there be this much magic in one town and none of the humans know?'

'We're good at keeping ourselves to ourselves.' Spencer shrugged. 'We just want to live our lives the same way humans do. Drama-free. It's only demons that seek out trouble wherever they go.'

'Good creatures of Crowood Peak,' Amethyst addressed the audience, who were still shuffling and murmuring but seated now. 'We welcome you and your families to town and to this gathering tonight. We're delighted to see you, but we do have important information for you – information about why you moved to Crowood Peak in the first place.'

Amethyst paused. 'You were lured here under false pretences.' Murmurs rumbled through the crowd.

'What do you mean?' said Birch. 'We came here because we found the perfect house.'

'And who sold you that house?' Emerald asked.

'Well . . . we were approached by an estate agent,' he said.

Bellamy smiled. 'Lovely woman.'

'A woman in a red suit with a white belt and white shoes?' Spencer asked.

'That's the one!' Birch clicked his fingers in recognition. 'You know her?'

'She sold us our house in Crowood too,' said Spencer.

Harriet raised her hand. 'And ours.'

'Did anyone else get approached by this "estate agent"? Did anyone else just happen to find the perfect house to live in here, whether you wanted to move or not? And did you find yourself agreeing to move without a moment's doubt or hesitation?'

Sheepishly, nearly everyone slowly raised their hand, and Maggie and Ivy assumed the handful that didn't were trying to save themselves embarrassment.

'So what is going on?' a voice called out.

'Someone better explain immediately.' A man in the middle of the hall stood up. He wore a long black coat, his features sunken but still sharp, and his long red hair exceedingly familiar.

'We will,' Amethyst assured him. 'Please bear with us, Mr . . . ?'

'Sparrow.' The man looked at Spencer. As did the rest of the Double Trouble Society.

Amethyst cleared her throat loudly. 'A long time ago, a witch used to live in this town. She was kind and helpful, but when she refused the marriage proposal of a demon, he cursed her and filled her heart with darkness and evil. She then begged him to let her live forever so she could continue her reign of terror for the rest of time. In order to grant that particular wish, she would need to eat the hearts of thirteen children before the next blue moon. She succeeded in luring and killing twelve children from Crowood Peak, but she failed to find the thirteenth. When the blue moon arose, she turned to dust. The curse was then passed to the next witch in the bloodline.'

'That was me.' Emerald raised her hand.

'But last year,' continued Amethyst, 'with the help of these wonderful children, we broke that curse.'

'Now we believe that the demon has come to seek his revenge,' said Emerald. 'He's brought all manner of creatures that thrive on dark magic to Crowood Peak. He wants to create an army, and we believe he'll strike at the next full moon.'

'Have you any proof?' Mr Sparrow said, crossing his arms and peering down his nose.

'That estate agent you met when you bought your house here.' Amethyst addressed the entire crowd, not just Spencer's father. 'Do you remember what colour eyes she had?'

All the adults shook their heads, utterly bemused as to why she'd ask such a trivial question and even more confused as to why they couldn't picture the face of the estate agent at all.

'Black!' Harriet's baby brother shouted and clapped his hands. 'Black eyes! Shiny! Shiny!'

'That's right, Rex,' cooed Harriet. 'She had black eyes. Because she was a demon. *The* demon.'

'You don't remember because adults, no matter what species they are, very rarely do. But children are more sensitive to demons,' Amethyst explained. 'All of your children who met the estate agent remember her black eyes and had nightmares for weeks on end after they met her.'

'They're right, Dad. Listen to them.' Behind him, Spencer could see his father getting more and more agitated. 'My father hates to be made a fool of,' he whispered to the gang. 'If that's what this demon has done by making him move here, he'll be furious.'

'I don't believe it!' Mr Sparrow boomed.

'We do have a little more proof, although this may be trickier to believe.' Amethyst didn't seem nervous, but the way she fiddled with the frayed end of a tassel on her purple dress gave her away. 'The ghosts of Crowood have awoken. It seems whatever this demon has been doing has disturbed the dead and roused their spirits. They're here in the school now.'

Orville spoke up. 'My great-times-eight-uncle was one of the twelve children killed by the Crowood Witch, and he's been haunting me since I arrived in this town.'

There was a moment of silence when everyone simply blinked at Orville. Then laughter that started with Spencer's dad rippled outwards until almost every single member of the crowd was guffawing loudly.

'Ghosts?!' Spencer's dad bellowed. 'GHOSTS!' He could barely contain himself.

'Wait, so werewolves and vampires are happy to accept that the other exists, but ghosts is where they draw the line?' said Orville in disbelief.

'Listen to the boy!' cried Bellamy. 'We are necromancers, and the spirit world is real.'

Birch nodded. 'I can feel the presence of many ghosts in this place.'

'Poppycock! Balderdash! Nonsensical ribaldry!' boomed Mr Sparrow.

'It seems the humans might be the least of our worries.' Eddie put his head in his hands.

'We believe in the *living*,' Bruce Harper said gently, chuckling away. 'But the dead are dead.'

'Well, unless you're undead . . .' Linda nudged Bruce and gestured to Spencer's father behind them.

He shrugged. 'That's different!'

'How? *How* is that different, Dad?' Harriet protested.

'Yes, I'd also like to know,' Bellamy snapped. 'We've spent our entire lives talking to the dead. We've solved hundreds of complex cases by doing what we do!'

'I'm not impressed by the number of people you've managed to deceive!' Mr Sparrow spat.

'We have photographic evidence!' shouted Orville. 'Surely you can't ignore that?'

He produced the photo of the Double Trouble Society and the ghost of Orin Thomas and thrust it into the hands of the man beside him in the front row. The man looked at it for a moment with interest, and then, raising an eyebrow at Orville, he passed it along the row. One by one, everyone examined the picture. Some dismissed it outright as a fake without so much as a glance, but others studied it for a good few minutes before handing it on.

'You can't truly expect us to believe this?' said Spencer's father.

'Dad, please!' Spencer pleaded.

'Hear them out, for goodness' sake!' shouted Bellamy. 'Something has clearly spooked this pair of fine witches. I'm sure they wouldn't have brought us all here for nothing.'

Amethyst was about to thank him when Spencer's dad threw up his hands, grumbled and began to make his way out of his row.

'LOOK!' someone near the back of the hall shouted. A woman was pointing with a long slender finger at the blackboard behind the two witches. They turned to see that a piece of chalk was hovering in mid-air and beginning to write.

WE ARE THE TWELVE. WE BELIEVE THE WITCHES.
THE DEMON IS COMING.
ORIN THOMAS

'That's enough proof for me!' said Birch.

'Parlour tricks! It's all smoke and mirrors!' Spencer's father yelled, gesticulating at Orville and the other children, who were growing red in the face with frustration. Then the lights in the school hall began to flicker, slowly at first and then more rapidly. Everyone had to shield their eyes or close them completely.

'What on EARTH is going on in here!!!' boomed a voice that not a single one of the children was pleased to hear.

'Mrs Stern,' Amethyst said with an exasperated sigh. A human adult in their midst was the very last thing she needed. 'You agreed to let us hold a meeting in the school hall this evening. Y'know . . . for our book club?' She squinted, holding up her hand to shield her eyes from the lights as they continued to buzz and flicker on and off, faster and faster.

Mrs Stern tottered over in her heels with ferocity. Her cheeks were getting pinker and pinker, a colour that she would have deemed far too frivolous and flamboyant to have anywhere on her person. A colour she'd sneered at Ivy for wearing to school each day.

'I agreed to a meeting!' Mrs Stern said, clenching her jaw, not letting the words escape easily. 'Not a . . . a . . . RAVE! Who's doing that with the lights?'

'It's not us, Mrs Stern!' Ivy said quickly. She didn't want another detention, even if she hadn't stuck around for the first one.

'Well then, WHO?!' bellowed the headmistress, not wanting to give in and close her eyes, but beginning to find it difficult as the lights grew brighter and brighter. Eventually, she had to clap her hands over her eyes.

The lights hissed before shattering altogether. Glass began to rain down around them, so Amethyst cast a quick spell to turn it into bubbles before the shards could hurt anyone. A hush fell over the hall.

'Is everyone OK?' Linda asked, her arms thrown protectively over her head.

'Yes, no thanks to that pair of cauldron-stirrers over there!' Mrs Stern spat, trying desperately to smooth her hair back into place. 'I don't know what you're playing at, but you two are never to set foot in this school again.' She turned and strode from the room, but not before slipping a little on the floor that was wet from all the bubbles.

'Come on, darling,' Spencer's father said to his wife, 'we're leaving too. Spencer, come.' Mr Sparrow clicked his fingers and pointed to the empty space by his side that his son was meant to fill.

'No, Dad,' Spencer said without a moment's hesitation. 'This is important, and my friends need your help. *I* need your help.'

'Sweetheart?' Spencer's mother's voice rang out for the first time. It was strong and commanding. She put her hand on Mr Sparrow's arm. 'We're in,' she announced.

Spencer's father swayed at her touch, grumbled and then sat down with a sigh. Mrs Sparrow looked at her husband with a defiant grin.

'If this all goes horribly wrong,' he muttered, 'don't come crying to me.'

Spencer smiled happily, and for a moment his father's lips turned upwards at the corners. If you'd blinked, you would have missed it.

20
The Witches Change

Preparations began immediately. When the sun came up the next day, Maggie and Ivy, still in their pyjamas and slippers, walked in the front door of Hokum House to the smell of burnt sugar and plums, and they knew Amethyst was cooking up some serious magic in her cauldron.

'I've decided to make a fresh batch of every potion I think might help us in the coming battle. There are strength potions, invisibility potions, potions that can temporarily make you fly, potions that can shrink you down or make you six metres tall. Everything I could possibly think of is being made.'

'Girls, I'd like to speak to you for a moment!' Emerald called from the garden.

Maggie and Ivy trotted out, rubbing the sleep from their eyes. They followed the path down to Emerald's little vegetable patch, where she was sitting in one of her long vibrant green dresses. She had woven a chain of little orange flowers into her hair and looked cheerful, despite the circumstances. Being in the garden always seemed to have a calming effect on her, and the longer she was out there, connecting with the earth and the grass, the better she felt.

'Now, I've been doing an awful lot of thinking, and what I'm about to say I do not say lightly. Amethyst and I have talked it over, and we've decided that none of the adult humans in this town should be involved in the fight.'

Maggie and Ivy rubbed at their eyes again, still blinking away their dreams. 'Amethyst is going to cast a spell to put all the humans to sleep the day that the next full moon is due to appear. They'll sleep soundly and, more importantly, *safely* in their beds while we do what we need to do.'

'Not *all* the humans, though, right?' Ivy asked. Emerald couldn't quite look her in the eye, and therein was Ivy's answer. 'You're not going to let Dad and Max help!' she yelped.

'No way!' Maggie gasped. 'They'll be furious!'

'They won't have a choice,' Emerald said firmly. 'For the sake of the anonymity of all the creatures that live here now, it isn't fair to expose them to an entire town's worth of humans who may or may not accept them for who they are.'

'We accepted you!' Maggie cried.

'I know, sweet girl, but not everyone did, and even now not everyone has. There are shops in the town square we're banned from. There are places we go where the whispers and looks make us feel so unwelcome that we have to leave anyway. We don't want to force that upon anyone else. Especially not the families of friends. Once this fight is over, these creatures may choose to leave Crowood Peak.'

'And anyway, in a fight against evil the humans won't be any use!' said Maggie.

'We're human,' Ivy said in a small voice.

'But you're children,' Emerald said, her eyes twinkling. 'Children see things that adults miss. You noticed that Spencer was a vampire and Harriet was a werewolf long before we even sensed their presence in this town. And Orville knew a ghost was following him, and it was the Double Trouble Society that discovered his identity. We *need* you.'

So Amethyst made potion after potion. She darted round the kitchen at what felt like a hundred miles per hour, sorting jars and vials and odd-shaped glass containers. Slowly, throughout the day, they were filled with liquids of every colour and consistency the girls could think of and even some colours they didn't know existed!

Emerald grew trees as tall as she possibly could and made walls of thorns as high as they were wide all the way round Crowood Peak. Together with the other magic users in town, she and Amethyst cast protection spells. They weren't sure how effective they'd be against this demon, but something was better than nothing. Amethyst tracked the phases of the moon more ardently than usual, testing her magic each night and feeling it get stronger and stronger as more of the moon became visible.

'I love the feeling just before a full moon. It's like my magic knows it's about to get supercharged. I can feel it bubbling beneath my skin. It's exactly how I need it to behave if we're about to face a demon.'

But the next morning everything changed.

Maggie and Ivy sat downstairs in Hokum House, happily eating toast. It was a Sunday and they'd forgiven Amethyst and Emerald for essentially implying that humans were useless the day before. There was too much to do to stay angry for long – what with a demon on his way and a town to save.

'They've slept in late,' Ivy said, peering up at the creaking floorboards above them. Amethyst and Emerald were early risers, sometimes even beating the sun. The girls could usually see purple smoke billowing from the chimney of Hokum House by the time they woke in the morning – Amethyst brewing a potion – and spot Emerald pottering about in the garden, but today the witches were nowhere to be seen.

'Maybe they're getting as much sleep as they can before the full moon tonight?' Maggie said, smothering her toast with lashings of marmalade.

'Something just doesn't feel quite right.' Ivy shuddered slightly. 'Maybe we should go and see if they're OK?' But just then the top stair creaked in the way it always did when someone was on their way downstairs.

'Girls?' Amethyst's voice sounded strange.

'Amethyst? Is everything OK? You sound . . . weird.'

'It's like she's sucked helium out of a balloon,' Maggie whispered, and Ivy nodded in agreement. Amethyst's voice was high and strangled. The two girls could also hear a faint sobbing and sniffling coming from the stairs.

'Something's happened,' Amethyst said. 'Emerald and I are fine, but we . . . well . . . we have a problem.' Her voice wobbled as she tried to keep her cool.

Maggie and Ivy left their breakfast and went to the bottom of the stairs. At the very top step were Amethyst and Emerald, but not as Maggie and Ivy had ever seen them before. The witches were children again.

'Why do you look like you're the same age as us?' Maggie asked, and Emerald started to sob.

'Because we are,' said Amethyst. 'Well . . . at least our bodies are.'

'It's the demon! It's his big trick before the fight!' Emerald threw her head back and wailed.

'It's OK! We'll manage! People will still take you seriously, even though you're kids!'

'It's not that, Maggie,' Amethyst said sadly.

'Then what is it?' Maggie scratched her head.

'Maggie, look at their hair,' Ivy whispered.

It was less noticeable with Amethyst's hair as it had gone from platinum-moon white to blonde, but Emerald's hair was now black.

'W-what . . . does that mean?' Maggie's lip began to wobble. Seeing the witches young was weird, but seeing them without their magic was hard. It was like looking at a tree without its leaves or the night sky without the moon.

'It means,' Emerald sniffed, 'that all our magic . . . it's GONE!'

'The demon has taken us back to the ages we were before we came into our powers. When he comes tonight, we'll be totally defenceless.' Amethyst was clearly trying to keep calm, but tears were coursing down her cheeks.

'I can't sense it at all, sister.' Emerald was rubbing her fingertips together, desperate to feel even a tiny tingle of magic beneath her skin. 'Not even the slightest trace.'

'I know. Me neither.' Amethyst's voice caught in her throat.

'H-how do you both feel?' Ivy asked.

'Empty,' they both said together.

'I know you might not think humans can be much use,' Maggie said, shooting a look at Emerald, 'but right now we need the help of grown-ups that we trust.'

They called Max and Bill to invite them over, and once they were all sitting round the kitchen table with tea and biscuits, the two men looked at the young witches curiously.

'I've not seen either of you in the Double Trouble meetings before.' Max squinted at Emerald, as if trying to place where he'd seen her face.

'No, nor have I, but you do look familiar. Do you have siblings that might be in the same class as our daughters?' Bill took off his glasses, cleaned them on the hem of his shirt, but when they were back on his nose he still shook his head.

'Dad.' Maggie rolled her eyes.

'What?'

'*Daaad*,' said Ivy.

'Are we being really silly and missing something incredibly important?' asked Bill, and Maggie and Ivy nodded.

Bill looked closer still. He noted Amethyst's impossibly straight and dazzlingly white teeth and the scattering of freckles over Emerald's nose. Max noticed that the dresses they were wearing were similar garments to ones he'd seen before, but they swamped these girls' small frames. Bill then suddenly realized if he changed their hair colour to green and platinum white they'd look awfully like . . .

'Oh my giddy aunt,' he said. 'How? How has this happened?'

'Wait for Dad to catch up . . .' Maggie held up a finger to Bill, who turned to Max. He was still gazing, puzzled, at the two new girls. It was only when he noticed they were wearing purple and green that the little connection in his brain ignited.

'NO WAY!' he said, slamming his fists on the table.

The young witches sighed. 'Way.'

'We're going to be totally useless when the demon arrives!' Emerald cried.

'Demon?!' Bill gulped.

'Hang on. I know this story. Demon curses witch. Witch's family and friends break curse. Demon wants revenge.' Max waited for someone to nod, and when Emerald acknowledged that his theory was spot on, he put one finger on his nose and pointed the other at Emerald.

'How did you know?' she asked.

Max shrugged. 'That's how all good stories go.'

'But how does it end?' Maggie asked, her eyes wide and hopeful.

'Well, darling, when I write my books, good always triumphs over evil, but sometimes the world doesn't work that way, I'm afraid.' Max put his arm round the back of Maggie's chair and she sank into his side a little.

'This time it will.' Ivy gave a firm nod and rose from her seat.

'It will?' said Amethyst, sniffing.

'It has to. We love Crowood and everyone who lives here too much to give it up without a fight. I think our love for this town is much stronger than the demon's desire to destroy it.' None of them had ever seen Ivy so riled up before.

'Right, I think you'd better fill us in on what's been happening. I get the feeling we've missed quite a bit,' Max said.

Several ginger biscuits and three pots of tea later, Ivy and Maggie had told Max and Bill the whole story. They were looking pretty shell-shocked.

'Vampires and werewolves . . . in Crowood Peak?!' Bill said, looking around nervously. 'Well, what do we do now?'

Ivy shook her head and sighed. 'I'm not sure, but whatever we do, we're going to need the help of *everyone* whether they're magical or not.'

21
Help Arrives

Everyone was gathered at Hokum House . . . creatures, humans and, of course, the Double Trouble Society. It was an odd mix of people, and lots of them looked delighted to be meeting the newcomers to the town. Mrs Moody, the librarian, was having a whale of a time chatting to a siren who now lived on Leaf Crunch Lane, and Mr Woodman was laughing at a joke Harriet's mum had just told.

Mrs Stern and Mr Sparrow were standing in the corner of the room, glaring at everyone, but no one seemed to take any notice of them and continued chatting to their neighbours, wondering why they'd been summoned to Hokum House at such short notice.

Ivy stood up on the coffee table and did a three-sixty spin, hushing the crowd to get everyone's attention, and silence fell quickly over the onlookers. Just as Ivy took a breath, ready to speak, the doorbell rang. Amethyst gestured for Ivy to carry on, and she left the room to answer the door.

'Hello, everyone. Thank you for coming. I'm sure there are lots of people in this room you've never seen before, and I hope you've used the time before I started speaking to get acquainted . . . Well –' she looked over at the stony faces of Mrs Stern and Mr Sparrow – 'anyway, what I'm about to say may come as a bit of a shock, but . . . er . . . here it is. Half the people in this room aren't exactly human. They're creatures like vampires, werewolves, warlocks and witches . . .'

'Siren,' said the woman chatting to Mrs Moody.

'Faun,' said a man standing awkwardly in the corner, scratching his legs agitatedly.

'Fairies!' said a group of small voices, but, when everyone looked around to see where they had come from, no one could spot the source.

'Gorgon,' said a woman sitting in Emerald's armchair. She had a black headscarf that shimmered green in the light, wrapped tightly round what, judging by the hissing sound coming from underneath it, was actually a nest of snakes. She wore the darkest of sunglasses, and as she got up and moved through the crowd everyone backed away a little and averted their gaze, just in case they accidentally caught her eye and were turned to stone.

'There are so many different types of people here, but today we're gathering for one common cause. To defeat a demon.'

'A what?' Miss Lightfoot asked. She was still dressed head to toe in Halloween clothes. Despite her evident love of the macabre, she seemed to shudder at the word 'demon'.

'There's a demon coming to Crowood Peak. Tonight when the full moon rises,' Emerald explained.

'WHAT? Who even is this child? Who does she belong to? I've never seen her at my school,' Mrs Stern spat, folding her arms across her chest.

'That's a lot to explain, and we don't really have time, so you're going to have to trust us, but . . . that's Emerald, Mrs Stern. One of the two witches who live in this house,' said Maggie.

Mrs Stern blinked and then let out what they all assumed was a laugh, but it sounded strangled and strange as if she wasn't used to laughing.

'We need your help. *Everyone's* help.'

'What can we do?' said Mr Woodman. He gave an apologetic shrug. 'I'm just a regular bloke. I don't have any of that fancy magic. Don't even have super strength! I can build a nice shed and put up a shelf or fix a leaky tap. I even make a great cuppa, but defeating a demon?'

Ivy smiled. 'Don't give up yet. I know there's only a handful of people in this room, but . . . but . . . I reckon if we all came together we'd be able to . . . to . . .'

Just as Ivy was beginning to lose faith, loud voices filtered in through the open door. She tried to continue, but the noise was getting louder and louder.

'Ivy, Maggie,' Amethyst's young voice trilled from the hallway. 'You're going to want to see this.'

The Double Trouble Society all looked at each other and then ran to the doorway, squeezing and shoving to get through it and into the hall. Amethyst stood in the way of the open door, blocking the view of what was behind her. Who could it be?

Trick or treaters? Ivy thought.

Early Christmas carollers? Maggie wondered.

Even more demons and scary monsters come to kill us? Harriet shuddered.

'It seems word has got out about the demon,' Amethyst explained. She was grinning from ear to ear.

'There's more people coming to help?'

'Oh *yesssss* . . .' she said. 'Just a handful.'

She finally stepped aside, and Ivy and Maggie couldn't believe their eyes. The street leading up to Hokum House was full of people they'd never seen before. No, not people. *Creatures*. Magical ones, their magic filling the air like a delicious haze, the smell of burnt sugar thick like fog.

'Look!' Maggie pointed at the sky, where it seemed there were more witches than stars above them. Some were waving at Maggie and Ivy as they hovered on their brooms. Others demonstrated their flying skills by doing expertly executed loop-the-loops and leaving glittering trails of sparkling colours behind them.

'Wow!' Ivy gasped, pointing further down the line, where a horde of ogres stood head and shoulders above the rest of the crowd, tusks protruding from their mouths, which would have been frightening had they not been grinning.

By this time, everyone in the house had made their way outside to witness the incredible crowd gathered to help their cause. All these creatures who had united and were going to fight for good, whether their magic was light or dark.

Amethyst and Emerald found each other among the happy chaos, held hands and spun in a circle, laughing.

'There's enough magic here to defeat an entire underworld of demons, never mind just one!' cried Emerald.

'We can still help,' said Mr Woodman, nodding slowly. 'At least . . . we want to.'

'We absolutely do!' said Miss Lightfoot, rolling up her puffy orange sleeves.

'Ridiculous. Nonsense.' Mrs Stern stumbled from the doorway, her mouth flapping open and closed as her eyes almost popped out of her head. 'Who are all these people?' She clawed at their clothes as she wobbled past them, her high heels sinking into the grass. 'Hired actors? You hired them, didn't you?' she said, clutching the lapels of Bill Eerie's shirt.

The tallest woman Maggie and Ivy had ever seen had begun to wander over to Mrs Stern. She must have been about eight feet tall and wore the most beautiful dress covered in tiny flowers and vines. It was only once she got closer that the girls noticed that the flowers and vines were real. When her bare feet touched the grass, flowers shot up all around them. Her hair was bright red and so long it swished and swayed and covered most of her face as she walked.

She stopped right in front of Mrs Stern, her shadow engulfing her, then knelt beside her so they were roughly the same height. Mrs Stern was shaking so badly they could hear her teeth chattering. Then the woman reached up a hand to her face and moved her red hair out of the way to reveal not two eyes, but one! Right in the centre of her forehead.

'Boo,' she said in a low voice. Mrs Stern let out the highest, shrillest, most blood-curdling shriek any of them had ever heard . . . and promptly fainted.

'Whoops!' the Cyclops boomed. 'Was that a little harsh?' She stood to her full height and smiled the most breathtaking of smiles with her beautiful pink lips.

'Nothing she didn't have coming. I think it's best she remains unconscious for what's about to happen,' Amethyst said, watching intently as Harriet's parents dragged Mrs Stern back inside the house.

'Yes, I think if she can't handle a Cyclops, she'll have real trouble with a demon.'

'A Cyclops! Wow!' Isaac pushed Maggie out of the way to get a closer look.

'Awesome! Does that mean you see differently to us?' Ivy asked, ever the scientist.

'It does! Cyclops's eyes protrude further, and are far larger, which means we can see peripherally much more than humans. Although we can only see in black and white.'

'Amazing!' Ivy said, gazing hard at the woman. The Cyclops moved her hair out of the way so Ivy could get a closer look. She looked left to right and up and down, and Ivy followed every move her pupil made.

'I'm Iris, by the way.' She held out a hand that completely engulfed Ivy's and Maggie's.

'It's a pleasure!' they said.

'No, no, the pleasure is all mine. I know this demon of old, and if there's a chance to stick it to him then I'm onboard.'

'It's good to have you here, Iris. Welcome to Crowood Peak.' Amethyst smiled.

How touching, said a voice. It was a low whisper, but it seemed to come from the very centre of Ivy's and Maggie's brains.

'Who said that?' Ivy whipped round, looking frantically for the source of the voice, but no one else seemed to have heard it.

'I can hear it too,' said Maggie.

One by one, the Double Trouble Society found each other and grasped one another's hands, trembling at the sound of the voice inside their heads. It was calm and steady, and yet underneath there was a fizzing excitement.

'What's happening?' Eddie asked, looking sideways at Spencer, who shrugged.

'It's the demon,' Ivy whispered. 'It has to be. We can hear him in our heads.'

'How do you know it's the demon?' asked Spencer.

'It's definitely him,' said Maggie, nodding and staring into the middle distance, feeling empty and desolate. (Demonic voices tend to have that effect on people.)

Just then, a low and vicious cackle slowly rose from the darkness of their minds and then it chanted in a sing-song way:

Come see me now in the place where you learn.
If not, you will see how the tables can turn.
Darla is here and Darla is fine,
But if you don't rescue her Darla is MINE!
Don't bring a spell, a potion or wand,
Or it's goodbye to those of whom you are fond.

If you aren't here when the clock strikes the hour,
Poor little Darla will soon feel my power.
Don't tell a soul. If you do, I will know.
I'm hiding, you're seeking: three, two, one . . . GO*!*

'He's got Darla?!' Sobs began to wrack Jennifer's chest.

'The place where we learn?' Maggie looked at Ivy. 'Why would he want us to go to the school?'

'He clearly wants us alone,' Ivy said.

'Not you. Us.' Emerald appeared hand in hand with Amethyst, pushing through the throngs of creatures all greeting each other.

'You heard the demon too?' Maggie asked, and they both nodded solemnly.

'He wants me and Emerald alone and unguarded by all this magic,' Amethyst explained. 'Now that we no longer have our powers, the demon knows we won't stand a chance against him.' They looked round at the magic that was now visible in the air, glittering all about them. 'He knows his own magic is completely and utterly outclassed if he comes to meet us here.'

'Instead, he's trying to lure us somewhere he can defeat us and get his revenge,' said Emerald.

'Then why don't we just stay here?' Isaac said with a shrug.

Jemima batted him with the back of her hand. 'We can't leave Darla with the demon!'

'And we won't.' Amethyst sucked in a deep breath, gripping Emerald's hand even tighter.

'We're going to go to the school and . . . and give ourselves up.'

'No way! We're coming with you, and we're going to defeat that demon together,' said Ivy, taking Amethyst's other hand.

'We can help you,' Eddie said, rolling up his sleeves.

'You can't,' said Ivy sadly. '*Don't bring a spell, a potion or wand, or it's goodbye to those of whom you are fond*,' she repeated.

'What does that even mean?' said Isaac in disgust.

'It means, dummy,' said Jemima scornfully, giving Isaac a painful nudge with her shoulder, 'that if we go with anyone who's a werewolf –' she pointed at Harriet – 'or a vampire –' she jabbed a finger at Eddie and Spencer – 'the demon will probably, more than likely, most definitely, vaporize Darla and the rest of us on the spot.'

Jennifer rolled her eyes. 'Thanks for that, Jemima.'

'What? I'm just being realistic!'

'In fairness, that is what the demon said,' said Maggie, and Jemima poked her tongue out at Jennifer.

'All right! I'm just saying I don't particularly like talking about my best mates being turned to dust by a demon from the fiery pits of hell!'

'She's right, though. Eddie, Spencer, Harriet . . . you can't come with us.' Ivy shook her head, unable to look any of them in the eye.

'What?!' snapped Eddie.

'Oh, come *on*!' Spencer said indignantly.

When Harriet didn't say anything, both young vampires looked at her with raised eyebrows, expectantly awaiting her response.

'I'm happy to sit this one out actually . . .' she said sheepishly, picking loose thorns off her leather jacket.

'We aren't leaving you to fight this demon alone,' Eddie said, defiantly clenching his fists and puffing out his chest.

'We're not alone. We have each other,' said Ivy.

'But you're . . . you're . . .' Spencer, lost for words, just wildly flailed his hands about, gesturing to the rest of the group.

'What? Human?' Ivy snarled.

'Well . . . yeah!' said Spencer. 'You're flesh and blood and bone. One spell would shoot right through you.'

'A spell would shoot through you too, Spencer,' Jemima taunted. 'I'm pretty sure vampires aren't impervious to a demon's magic.'

'No, we might not be *impervious* –' Spencer mimicked her voice – 'but I'm pretty sure the fact that we can turn into bats and *fly* might give us more of an edge! We can dart about and dodge whatever he tries to throw our way!'

'We'll show you that humans aren't helpless at all,' said Maggie, wagging her finger in the young vampire's face.

'We will?' Jamie said, his hands beginning to tremble.

'Yeah. We're gonna defeat this demon all on our own,' Jemima hissed, keeping her voice low, making sure no one around them heard.

'Is this a good idea?' Emerald whispered to Amethyst.

'No. Not at all. But you heard what the demon said. *If you aren't here when the clock strikes the hour, poor little Darla will soon feel my power.*' Emerald gulped as Amethyst repeated the demon's words. 'We have no choice. Either we go alone and try to defeat the demon with no magic, and he kills us, or we don't go at all, and he kills Darla and most likely everyone else anyway!'

'Maybe this adventure is a little scarier than last year's, eh?' Maggie said to Ivy, trying to chuckle, but it didn't come out at all.

'Definitely,' Ivy said, squeezing Maggie's cold fingers. 'But even if this is our last adventure we're going out with a bang. And no one can say we weren't brave.'

'The bravest, I'd say.' Maggie nodded. 'Now we need a distraction. Something that will make everyone look in one direction while we run towards the school. We can't risk anyone here following us.'

'*AAAARRROOOOOOOO!*' Harriet suddenly howled as loud as she could. 'Help me! I don't feel right! I think the demon's magic has got hold of me!'

She clutched at her throat, tore at her jacket and tugged at her hair as if she was being driven mad by something no one else could see. For a brief moment, her eyes flicked to Maggie's and Ivy's, and she gave them a wink. Then she turned and dashed away from the Double Trouble Society and into the crowd of magical creatures whose eyes were fixed on her. Eddie and Spencer hurried after her.

'Help! Help! I can hear the demon inside my head! He's got hold of us too!' yelled Eddie.

'Well, that'll work,' Maggie said, turning towards the school and beginning to run. '*Go! Go! Go!*'

22
Ink and Fog

They ran, feet pounding the pavement, chests heaving and throats frosting over with their icy breath. The closer they got to the school, the darker the sky became. Not in the way that clouds turn a darker grey just before a storm, blending gradually from one colour into the next. No, this was a firm and definitive line in the sky. As if someone had taken a black marker, drawn a line and only coloured in one side. The clouds went from white and fluffy to black as coal and as thick as smoke. When they reached the end of the road their school was on, it was as if the light was being sucked out of everything. They could barely see their own hands in front of their faces.

'Torches!' Maggie instructed.

Jamie, Jennifer and Jemima had torches on their school key rings. Only little ones that you had to keep pressed in order to shine, but they were extremely bright, and with all three of them on they were able to find their way. Maggie and Ivy both had proper torches in their coat pockets at all times. Isaac also had a decent torch in his rucksack for hunting for creepy-crawlies that only show themselves at night. Orville didn't have a torch, but he did have a digital camera with a flash that he could use to light his way.

Amethyst and Emerald took Maggie and Ivy's hands, and they ran ahead to scope out the area.

'Be careful!' Amethyst hissed into Maggie's ear. 'The demon could be anywhere!'

'How do we get through the gates?' Maggie asked, reaching out for Ivy as she stumbled.

'I don't think that's going to be a problem.' Ivy shone her torch on them.

The black wrought-iron bars were bent and misshapen. The chain that was usually wound round the centre bars to keep the gates together was lying broken on the ground, the padlock missing entirely. The words CROWOOD SCHOOL that sat on top of the gates, also in iron, now read CRO O S H OL.

The rest of the letters either hung at an angle, had swivelled upside down or had fallen off completely. As if the impact of something huge had loosened their screws and knocked them off kilter.

Ivy pushed one of the gates, and it opened with a *crrrreeeeeeaaaaakkkkk*. The sky rumbled overhead.

'I-i-is this such a good idea? Going in w-w-without . . . witch supervision?' Orville stuttered, looking warily at the black and writhing sky.

'Technically, we're still witches. We're just at a point in our timeline where we have no powers,' Emerald said, her bottom lip trembling.

'Remind me why we're here again? Completely and utterly defenceless and definitely about to be incinerated by demon magic?' Jemima asked, her tiny torchlight beginning to tremble.

'Because the demon has Darla, and we never leave any member of the Double Trouble Society behind,' said Maggie firmly.

Right above their school, the cloud looked like a bundle of snakes, their twisting, slippery bodies all tangled in the air. There was a hiss and a snarl, but it wasn't coming from the sky. It was coming from inside their heads. The gates were so heavy that they slammed shut with a deafening *CLANG* that rang in everyone's ears, but it still didn't drown out the voice of the demon in their heads.

No turning back now,
You've walked through the gates.
Please come and join me:
Your doom awaits.

There was a moment of silence when the rumbling in the sky quietened, the voice had ceased, and not one of them dared to breathe and break the stillness. Then, as quickly as it had come, the silence ended, and a deafening roar of wind blew against them so hard that they all had to lean into it to avoid getting knocked over.

'*AAARRRGHHH!*' they all yelled, grabbing on to one another.

The soles of their shoes could no longer grip the pathway beneath their feet. It was as if the ground was covered in grease. Their feet slid all the way down the path and right into the centre of the playground. The swings swung so violently that they flipped right over the bars again and again until there was no chain left to swing. The little roundabout whizzed round and round so fast the bolts holding the centre of it down rattled out of their holes, and the roundabout took off into the sky, slicing through the air like a UFO.

'HOLD ON TO EACH OTHER!' Ivy screamed over the uproar.

They tried to reach out, but the gale was far too furious. Tendrils of thick black fog descended from the sky, slithering across the playground, low to the ground, weaving this way and that. First the fog found Jennifer before she was able to lift her torch. It wound its way round her legs and circled her body until she was completely encased.

'Hello?!' Jennifer blinked, but there was nothing but darkness. She began to feel dizzy as she spun this way and that, trying desperately to make out her friends' voices. 'Why can't I see anything?! Where has everyone gone?'

Maggie and Ivy whipped their torches around to try and find Jennifer, but she'd completely disappeared. It was only when she started darting frantically in one direction and then another that they noticed the mass of fog moving across the playground.

'Just stand still, Jennifer! He's got me too!' Jemima called. Maggie and Ivy moved their torches towards the sound of Jemima's voice, but all they could see was another fog-covered shape.

'*Aargh!*' Spinning round, they saw Orville's face disappearing under the shadowy cloud, and Isaac soon followed.

Maggie and Amethyst ran over to Ivy and Emerald quickly and clutched their hands. 'If we keep together, then we'll get covered in fog together, and we can figure a way out together too!' Maggie yelled.

'Great plan!' The four of them linked arms at the elbows, squeezing each other tightly.

Silly little witches, the voice chuckled in their heads.

'What's that?' Maggie noticed something stirring in the doorway to the main school building. Something small and nimble, moving fast in the darkness, but, when Maggie shone her torch over it, it stopped.

'DARLA!' Maggie cried out and tried to run towards her, but Ivy's and Amethyst's arms were locked firmly round hers and she couldn't move. 'What are you doing? It's Darla!'

'I know it looks like Darla, but . . . is it?' Ivy couldn't take her eyes off the little girl.

'What do you mean? Ivy, you're being ridiculous!' Maggie hissed.

'No, she's not,' said Amethyst softly, staring at Darla. 'Look at her eyes.'

Maggie hadn't noticed before, but when she shone the torch at Darla she could see that the little girl's eyes were as black as night. Maggie sucked in a breath and her blood ran cold.

'Darla? What happened to you?' Ivy asked, her teeth beginning to chatter.

Darla's mouth opened, but the sound that came out wasn't her sweet little voice. It was different. Low and snarling and familiar. It was the voice they'd been hearing in their heads. The demon laughed, rolling the name around in his mouth like a hard-boiled sweet. '*Darla, Darla, Darla*. It seems that double the trouble doesn't necessarily mean double the brains.' He snickered.

'Tell us what happened to our friend,' Emerald spat, fighting against Amethyst's arms.

'I picked the youngest member of your silly little group because I knew she'd be the easiest to befriend and control. All it took was a measly bar of chocolate and she let me get close enough to possess her. Since you destroyed my curse, I knew I'd have to bide my time before seeking my revenge. I wanted to get close enough to learn your weaknesses. It was tough. You're both strong, but you've learned to rely on magic for everything. Without it, you have no idea how to confront me!' The demon laughed so loudly that the ground beneath their feet began to quake.

'Ivy, what are we going to do?' Maggie whispered out of the corner of her mouth.

They looked around frantically to see if there was anything that could help them. The demon's shadows were edging closer and closer, and everything was getting darker and darker. In seconds, it would all go black, and they'd be engulfed in fog. But then Ivy noticed something very, *very* important.

'The torches . . . *look*!' she hissed, pointing to where some of the Double Trouble Society's torches lay strewn across the playground, still creating bright beams and rings of light. The fog had swallowed the entire playground, a thick layer of it coating the tarmac and rising up round their friends. However, the fog hadn't touched the torches where the light shone. It was as if the darkness had tiptoed round the light, unwilling to touch it.

'The fog doesn't like the light, so we need to get to those torches. Amethyst and Emerald, you stick together, and I'll stay with Maggie. We split up. Ready?' Ivy adjusted her stance, one foot in front of the other, ready to run.

'What are you doing?' Demon Darla bellowed.

'Three . . . two . . . one . . .'

'STOP!' the demon roared.

'GO!' Ivy and Maggie ran to the left, and Amethyst and Emerald ran to the right as fast as they could, their legs scrambling beneath them, the inky shadows and charcoal fog hot on their heels. Maggie snatched the nearest torch off the ground, and she and Ivy spun round to face the fog. As the beam of light hit the grey clouds, it carved a pathway through it.

'Got one!' Emerald was also waving a torch around.

'We need to rescue the others! GO!' Ivy yelled.

'NO!' Demon Darla wailed. She began to grow bigger until she was towering over them, her eyes full of darkness. She looked nothing like their sweet friend any more. Darla tried to swipe at Maggie and Ivy, but she moved too slowly, and they easily darted out of the way. As they ran, Ivy snatched up another torch and spun in a circle, carving a large pathway in the fog.

'Use your torchlight to release the others!' she instructed, running to the nearest tornado of fog and shining her torch from its tippity-top all the way down to the bottom to reveal Orville. He was extremely pale and shivering, clutching his chest where his camera used to hang.

Demon Darla reached down and tried to grab Maggie as she released Jennifer and then at Amethyst who had freed Jemima and Isaac, but the bigger the demon became, the slower it moved. Maggie was able to quickly run out of the way.

'It seems I have outgrown poor little Darla.' It began to shrink back to Darla's normal size. 'I think it's time to change into something smaller and more nimble. Something with a little more . . . BITE!' The demon opened Darla's mouth and out of it poured hundreds and hundreds of . . .

'BATS!' Maggie screamed. 'RUN INTO THE SCHOOL AND DO NOT GET BITTEN!'

Ivy pulled her coat up round her head and used her torch to light the way as she ran as fast as her feet would carry her through the nearest door. She held it open as Orville, then Maggie, then Amethyst, then Emerald, then Jamie, then Isaac and finally Jennifer all sprinted through it.

Jemima was running as quickly as she could, but the bats were so close that they were nipping at her hair as it trailed behind her. '*AAARRRGGGHHH!*' she screamed as she hurtled inside.

As Ivy slammed the door shut, they could hear the thump of little bats pummelling the wood, unsuccessful in their mission to take a bite out of Jemima's neck. Jemima landed hard on her knees, grazing them on the floor of the school corridor.

They all ran over and pulled her up. She wobbled for a moment and tried to take a step forward.

'Ouch. My knees really hurt.'

'You may have broken something. You landed so hard, I think the ground shook!' said Jennifer.

'*Mmmmmm*,' someone groaned in agreement.

'That demon really is every bit as dreadful as everyone said.' Orville shuddered.

'*Mmmmmm*.' They groaned again.

'I don't reckon that's the end of it either. I think it's all about to get a whole lot worse,' added Maggie.

'*MMMMMMMM!*'

'Jamie, why are you making that weird noise?' asked Ivy.

Jamie screwed up his face in confusion. 'I'm not. I thought that was Jemima.'

'Don't look at me.' Jemima shrugged and then winced as she tentatively touched one of her grazed knees.

'Well, if wasn't any of us, then . . . who was it?' Isaac asked cautiously, unsure if he wanted to know the answer.

'*Mmm?*' A quizzical groan this time and it was clear it was coming from behind them. They all looked at each other, wide-eyed, and slowly turned towards the sound. Standing not far away was a boy. He was staring at them.

'Hello? Are you all right? Who are you?' Maggie asked, taking a few steps towards him.

'I don't have a good feeling about this,' Amethyst whispered.

'Maggie, come back!' Ivy reached out to grab the sleeve of Maggie's coat, but she shrugged her off.

'What's your name? Are you trying to get away from the demon too?' asked Maggie.

'*Mmmm.*' The boy groaned.

'Do you speak? Has the demon cut out your tongue?'

'*Maggieeeee*,' Ivy hissed urgently.

Maggie turned to her. 'Ivy, I'm just trying to make sure he's OK. We've seen what this demon is capable of, and this might be a kid from Crowood in need of our help.'

'*MAGGIE*.' Ivy's voice was a raspy whisper as she stared over Maggie's shoulder.

'What?' Maggie asked, but as she turned back to the boy she saw exactly what Ivy was talking about.

The boy had taken a few steps forward and was now directly in the light. They could see that his skin was grey with a bluish-purple hue. It had torn away in streaks like old worn leather, but the more disturbing feature on the boy's face was his left eye . . . It was hanging out of its socket and resting on his protruding cheekbone.

'ZOMBIE!' Maggie screamed, racing back to the group and herding them down the corridor. '*GO!*'

'*MMMMM!*'

Isaac looked back just in time to see the zombie boy dragging its stiff rigor-mortis legs in their direction.

'Faster!' he screeched, but then bumped into Jemima, who bumped into Jennifer, who bumped into Jamie, who bumped into Ivy and Maggie, who had stopped abruptly. Underneath the flickering fluorescent lights of the corridor, they saw an even more horrifying sight.

In front of them, filling the hallway, stood at least a hundred zombies, shoulder to shoulder, an army of the undead.

'It seems our demon has a grave-robbing hobby we didn't know about,' said Maggie.

'Back! Back! BACK!' Ivy hollered, and they turned and ran down the hallway, past the boy zombie, who, luckily for them, moved pretty slowly, and towards the school assembly hall.

Jamic looked over his shoulder. Their yelling had alerted the other zombies, who had started to move towards them. The Double Trouble Society burst through the doors, locked them quickly and then huddled together in the centre of the school hall. Hundreds of bats were swarming round the windows, flapping their wings and baring their fangs, desperate to get inside. With bats at the windows, zombies on the way and a demon desperate to destroy them, they were completely and utterly trapped.

23
Ivy Always Has a Plan

'What's the plan, Ivy?' Isaac asked.

'I . . . I . . . I don't know!' she croaked.

'What do you mean? You've always got a plan!' Jamie's voice broke with panic.

'I know, but I've never taken on a demon and an army of bats and zombies before. I don't know how to do this.' Ivy began to wring her sweaty hands.

'Yes, you do. You've got this. You've got *us*,' Maggie said, grabbing Ivy by the shoulders. 'You might be the brains, but we're a team. You aren't alone. Just tell us what we need to do, and we'll do it.'

Ivy's lip wobbled for a moment, but then there was a little spark in her brain.

'Jamie. You're in the school band, aren't you?' she said.

'Electric guitar player extraordinaire, at your service.' Jamie saluted.

'There are instruments in the school, right? In the music room maybe?'

'There's loads in the music room, but . . . my guitar's behind the stage. There's meant to be a recital after school tomorrow. My mum's dead excited!'

'I highly doubt that recital will be happening, Jamie.' Jemima rolled her eyes.

'Well, it definitely won't be if we don't hurry up!' Isaac tapped his watch.

'Is there an amp as well? How loud does it go?'

'Loud enough to wake the dead, Mum says.'

'Well, that's already happened,' said Ivy, thinking of the horde of zombies outside the hall. 'Go and get it!'

Jamie disappeared through a little door to the side of the stage and reappeared with his guitar case slung across his back, wheeling an amp towards them, the wire already plugged in and trailing behind him.

'That's perfect. OK, plug in your guitar and turn up the amp as loud as it will go,' Ivy instructed. 'Everyone else needs to head to a window and get ready to open it.'

'OPEN IT?!' Emerald cried.

'Ivy, have you totally lost it? There's, like . . . a bajillion bats outside!' Maggie shrieked.

'Yes, I'm not sure this is such a good idea.' Amethyst gently put her hand on Ivy's shoulder.

'Oh, Ivy, you're a genius!' Isaac had cottoned on to her plan. 'Jamie, you need to play the highest notes you can. And any feedback from the amp is good! The more the better.'

'I need you to trust me,' Ivy pleaded, taking Amethyst's hands in hers.

'She might not be a witch, and she doesn't have magic, but she has a brain and cleverness and, well . . . I think that *is* a kind of magic,' Maggie said.

Amethyst gave Ivy's hands a squeeze. She nodded. 'OK. Let's do this.'

'Everyone ready to open the windows?' Ivy asked, and they all gave her a thumbs up. Jamie, Jennifer and Jemima weren't sure what Ivy's plan was, but they trusted her implicitly, so they manned their windows all the same.

'OK, Jamie, start playing . . . NOW!'

Jamie began to shred the fretboard, playing no tune in particular, but making sure all the notes were as high as he could possibly play. Then he turned and faced his amp, which produced a high-pitched squealing sound. The Double Trouble Society flinched, desperate to cover their ears, but they didn't let go of the window latches.

'And open your windows . . . NOW!'

The windows swung open, and everyone ducked, ready for the onslaught of flapping wings and sharp biting gnashers . . . but nothing came.

Jennifer was the first to peek. There wasn't a bat in sight. With her hands firmly over her ears, she peered outside. The bats were flying in the opposite direction. 'Ivy! You did it!' But no one could hear her over Jamie's playing. Jennifer ran to him and jolted him out of his musical trance, the noise of his guitar coming to an abrupt end.

'Sorry! I got carried away. That was fun!' He high-fived Jennifer, who was grinning from ear to ear, even though her ears were ringing.

'Bats don't have great eyesight, but they have amazing ears that are incredibly sensitive to high frequencies and vibrations. Your guitar was enough to scare them off for a while at the very least,' Isaac explained. 'Nice one, Ivy!'

Ivy grinned, thrilled she'd managed to think quickly on her feet. Emerald ran to hug her.

'Well done! That was . . .'

'Magic!' Amethyst yelped, throwing her arms round them both.

BANG! The zombies were finally at the doors to the hall.

'OK. What about that lot?' Maggie jumped up and down and then cracked her knuckles, ready to take on the next challenge.

'I'm afraid I've got no idea how to get rid of zombies,' Ivy said. 'I think we're just gonna have to take them on ourselves . . .'

'Take them on ourselves?!' Jemima laughed hysterically. 'There are loads of them and only nine of us!'

BANG! BANG! BANG! The zombies were rattling the doors.

'Once they get in here, they're going to want to eat our brains!' Orville whimpered. 'We need to do something! Now!'

This time an idea sparked in Maggie's brain. 'Everyone get in a circle and hold hands! And don't break the circle.' She cleared her throat and closed her eyes. 'We call upon the ghost of Orin Thomas! Are you there?'

'Please be there! Please be there!' Orville whispered. Unlike the last seance, there was a response immediately. Maggie's torch began to flash on and off.

'Please help us in our time of need!' she yelled.

'All right, all right. No need to shout.'

Maggie opened her eyes and floating in the centre of the circle was the ghost of Orin Thomas himself. He was blue and wobbly around the edges, and his limbs seemed to blur when he moved, but it was definitely him.

'Uncle Orin?' said Orville softly.

Orin smiled. 'I'm guessing you need my help to rescue you from . . . well . . . me.' Orin grimaced towards the banging on the school hall doors.

'You?' Jennifer gasped.

'Oh no.' Ivy groaned, the realization dawning on her.

Orin continued. 'The demon's enlisted every single body buried in Crowood Peak into his army of the undead. That's why all our ghosts have returned.'

'But hang on . . . doesn't that mean he's accidentally awakened an army of ghosts too?' Amethyst asked.

'It absolutely does, and we are at your service.' Orin saluted. 'Soldiers!' he called, and all at once hundreds of ghosts floated up through the floors, down through the ceilings and in through the walls. 'It is our job to keep the Double Trouble Society safe from ourselves. Can we do that?'

'YEEESSS, SIIIIR!' they moaned back ghoulishly.

'*ARRRGGGGHHHHHHHHH!*' everyone shrieked.

The whole building began to shudder and shake. The ceiling panels started to crumble and fall down. The plaster of the walls cracked, and huge chunks of it fell away and landed on the floor.

'What's happening?!' yelled Ivy.

'Help us!' Maggie begged Orin, but he was already floating towards them. The ghosts had formed a human shield round and above the children, creating a ghostly dome to protect them from any falling debris. The Double Trouble Society looked up through their transparent bodies to see that the entire roof of the hall had been ripped off and, looming high above them, was the demon in his true form.

Not an estate agent. Not Darla. Not a horned devil. This was shadow and fog and ink. A creature made of pure darkness, with glowing eyes set back in his smoky face, burning like fires.

'I will NOT be defeated!' he roared. His voice was no longer in their heads and no longer in the mouth of a small child. It vibrated through every bone in their bodies and made their teeth ache in their skulls. The demon reached down into the school hall, his cloudy hands enveloping the dome of ghosts. He pushed down, the ghosts howling under the pressure.

'STOP IT!' Maggie cried. 'YOU'RE HURTING THEM!'

Emerald put a gentle hand on Amethyst's shoulder. 'He wants us,' she whispered.

'What? What do you mean?' said Maggie, overhearing her.

'We're the ones who broke his curse. He wants revenge on *us*. This isn't anyone else's battle. It's ours.'

'Of course it's *our* battle. We're your family. If he wants to get to you, he has to come through us first!' Maggie said, balling up her fists and readying herself to fight.

'Maybe you don't have to give yourselves up,' Ivy said, her eyes glimmering with a fresh idea. 'Maybe you just need to use yourselves as bait . . .'

'Keep talking,' said Amethyst.

'This demon might have an army of zombies and bats, but we have our own army waiting at Hokum House. Right now, we're outnumbered, and the ghosts can't keep us safe for long. But if the ghosts let us through their barrier –'

'We run back to Hokum House and lure him there . . .' Emerald said.

'We might actually stand a chance of defeating him!' Maggie finished.

'EXACTLY!' shouted Ivy.

'Right, ghosties.' Amethyst faced the dome of spirits. 'You need to let us through, but we need a few of you to shield us all until we get out of the building.'

Orin looked at them, wide-eyed, for a moment and then said, 'Whatever you say!' through gritted teeth as he strained against the strength of the demon.

The ghosts opened a pathway in front of them, creating a protective wall between the four of them and the others, preventing them from being attacked by the demon as they escaped.

'What are you doing?!' Orville yelled.

'You can't let him get us!' Jemima thumped her fist against the wall of ghosts, but one of them let out a moan, and she didn't try that again.

'Trust us,' Maggie said with a small smile. She wasn't entirely convinced that this would work, but they had no other options. More ghosts formed a smaller dome round them.

'Are you ready?' Ivy asked the ghosts, as well as the living. When everyone nodded, she yelled, 'RUN!' and they took off as fast as they could. All nine of them barrelled through the doors of the hall and barged down the corridor. The zombies hit the dome of ghosts like insects on a car windscreen and were tossed aside.

'NO!' the demon yelled as he saw them escape. They tore up the path and out of the school gates.

'I'm sorry!' Orin said. 'I can't leave the place I haunt!' Suddenly he was whipped back to the school like a stretched elastic band finally being released, and a few other ghosts went with him.

'It's OK!' Maggie shouted. They kept on running, the remaining ghosts close by their side until Hokum House was in sight.

'HELP! HELP US!' they yelled. The crowd of creatures began to turn their way, and Bellamy and Birch ran to them.

'Where on earth have you been? We've been so worried!'

'The demon lured us . . . to the school . . .' Emerald panted. 'Said he had Darla . . . but the demon *was* Darla . . . or had possessed her . . . it was a trap . . . and then there were zombies . . . and . . . and . . .'

'And now we need to fight. All of us. Together!' said Maggie.

24
The Battle of Hokum House

'How are we going to fight the demon without our magic?' Emerald said, wringing her hands.

Amethyst took Emerald's hands in hers. 'We might not have magic, but we're surrounded by it.'

'And we humans aren't completely useless either! Ivy, is the demon made out of the same fog that was in the playground?' Maggie asked.

Ivy thought for a moment, and then her eyes widened. 'BRILLIANT, MAGGIE! We have a plan!' She turned to face everyone and raised her voice. 'We need mirrors and reflective surfaces! As many as we can find, big and small.' Everyone simply stared at her.

'Well, don't just stand there!' Bellamy bellowed. 'Go and find the girl some mirrors!'

Fairies, ogres, gorgons, sirens, witches, vampires, warlocks, werewolves and the Double Trouble Society scattered all at once, tripping over themselves to find as many mirrors as they could. They raided Hokum House, tearing the bathroom and bedroom mirrors off the walls. They searched their own pockets for compact mirrors, and one ogre went down the street, wrenching the wing mirrors off all the cars.

'I don't condone vandalism, but . . . desperate times!' he said with a shrug.

Once everyone had something reflective in their hands, they ran back to Ivy. She instructed them all to group together and hold out their mirrors in the direction of the demon to create one giant reflective surface.

'Left a bit, Birch. Up a bit, Amethyst . . . We need it angled upwards so it's aimed right at the demon's chest. That's it! Perfect! Now hold still!'

Ivy looked behind her. The demon was lumbering towards them in great galumphing steps, his eyes smouldering like two fiery pits of hell. Ivy summoned the rest of the Double Trouble Society with a desperate wave of the hand.

'Torches! Aim them at the mirror everyone else has made! Ready, steady . . . NOW!'

They did exactly as she said and . . . nothing. There was a little bit of glare, but their torches just weren't strong enough. The demon was getting closer now. Some of the fairies had begun to shoot spells at him, but he simply swatted their magic away like gnats.

'We need more light!' Jemima shouted.

'Will this do!' Max's voice yelled out loud and clear. He was reversing his car out of their driveway. 'Come on, Bill!'

They turned to see Bill doing the same. Suddenly lots of cars were pulling out of their driveways along the street. They parked them in the middle of the road, facing the makeshift mirror. Bill and Max turned their headlights on, and Ivy jumped in the air while Maggie whooped.

'Yes, Dad!' Maggie threw up her fist in triumph.

'Full beams!' Ivy instructed. '*GO!*'

The light was so blinding that everyone had to shield their eyes. The headlights hit the mirrors, and the light refracted up at the demon. The demon roared and, as he opened his mouth, they could see a flaming fire inside it like a forked tongue. The light hit the demon full in the chest and the fog . . . disappeared! The light had created a hole and they could see the sky through it.

'Look!' Jennifer cried, pointing to Amethyst and Emerald.

The witches were no longer children. They were both at least thirty centimetres taller than they had been. Emerald's facial features were more pointy and Amethyst's were softer – but, more importantly, Emerald's hair was green and Amethyst's was white-blonde! They might not have been back to their normal grown-up selves, but they were past the point in their ages where they had come into their powers! Amethyst began to rub her hands together, creating purple sparks. Emerald did the same, and green flames started to lick out from between her palms.

'Move the mirrors! Try and angle the light so it gets rid of all the fog!' yelled Ivy.

'Make that demon disappear!' Eddie shouted.

The parents kept honking their horns as they watched Maggie and Ivy's plan in action. But the demon wasn't going to go without a fight, and he began to run. Just a few more of those enormous strides and he would be upon them. Amethyst and Emerald raced over to the rest of the Double Trouble Society and faced the mirrors.

'Ready, sister?' Amethyst said, her voice calm and confident. Emerald threw back her head and cackled a teenage-witch cackle.

'Oh, I'm always ready, sis.'

'NOW!' Ivy and Maggie screeched as the demon loomed over them. Emerald and Amethyst aimed their bright streams of magic right at the mirrors.

'STOP! STOP! STOOOOOOOOOOOOP!'

The demon begin to shrink, and he kept shrinking until he was the size of an ant. The gang watched him dart this way and that like an annoying fly.

'Ivy, Maggie, would you like to do the honours?'

'Eww . . .' Ivy said, scrunching up her face.

'I'll do it!' Maggie said.

Without hesitation, she stomped her foot down on the teeny-weeny demon and squashed him with a satisfying squelch. Right away, Amethyst and Emerald began to grow again, a haze of purple and green surrounding them. Once the colourful fog disappeared, they were all grown up and back to normal.

'Well, I don't think the demon will be bothering us again,' said Emerald.

Maggie examined the bottom of her shoe closely.

'Yuck! No, I don't think he will either,' she said, grinning.

25
The Battle is Over

After the demon was vanquished, everyone cheered and a street party began.

'I think this calls for some music!' Jamie held his guitar aloft.

As soon as he started playing, other people ran home to get their instruments, and a band formed in the middle of the street. And when music plays, dancing is sure to follow. Creatures and humans alike moved in between all the cars parked in the road, and the party continued long after the sky became dark.

Mrs Anderson rushed to the Cosy Cauldron and came back with as many cakes and cookies as she could carry.

When she realized there wasn't enough to feed everyone, Birch cast a multiplying spell until there were more sweet treats than anyone could possibly eat.

'Please tell me you're staying in Crowood Peak!' Mrs Anderson said, looking at him, doe-eyed. 'With magic that useful, there's a job for you at the Cosy Cauldron. Both of you!' she said as Bellamy joined them.

'D'you know what? I think Crowood Peak might just be a place we could call home.'

'Us too!' said Spencer's mother as she danced past in a conga line.

Even Mrs Stern appeared from Hokum House, having recovered from her faint, but she didn't stay for long. With a huff and a puff and a roll of the eyes, she took one look at the magical party and turned sharply on her heel. Magic, it seemed, would never quite win her over.

'Maggie, Ivy . . .' said a little voice.

Maggie and Ivy gasped as they looked down and saw Darla tugging at their sleeves. Her eyes were no longer black and her voice was back to its usual sweet and angelic tone.

'DARLA!'

Maggie scooped the little girl up in her arms, and the sound of her giggling alerted the rest of the Double Trouble Society, who came flocking to her. They hugged Darla tighter than ever before and gave her as many cookies as she could eat.

As the party drew to a close and everyone began to filter back to their homes, grinning from ear to ear, Maggie, Ivy, Bill, Max, Amethyst and Emerald sat on the grass in the front garden of Hokum House.

'I do wish this town didn't keep putting you two in positions that were quite so dangerous,' Bill said, throwing his arm round Ivy's shoulders and kissing the top of her head.

'Me too!' she said, giggling.

'At least it's all over now, and we can have five minutes' peace and a cup of tea. I think that's exactly what we need,' said Max.

'You did so well, girls,' Amethyst said with a smile. 'Your brain,' she told Ivy, 'and your bravery,' she said to Maggie, 'really are magic. I hope you know that.'

'Thanks. But I bet you're glad to have your actual magic back, though, right?' Maggie asked.

Emerald smiled, opening her palm as a little green flame sprang up from her skin and sizzled.

'Thank goodness for that!' Ivy exclaimed.

'As much as I'm glad we're grown-ups once more . . . it was fun being a child for a little while.' Emerald looked at her sister with a twinkle in her eye.

Max sighed. 'Ahh, what I wouldn't give to be a kid again for just one night.'

'Oh, me too! Wouldn't that be fun!' Bill smiled as he looked up at the night sky speckled with stars.

Emerald grinned. 'Hey, Amethyst, are you thinking what I'm thinking?'

'RACE YA!' Amethyst hopped up off the grass and grabbed Bill by the hand.

'Not fair! You had a head start!' Emerald laughed as she took hold of Max and hauled him to his feet. Maggie and Ivy giggled. Only a few moments later, the two witches came speeding round the side of the house on their brooms.

'*WAAAAHHHOOOOOOOO!*' Max sat behind Emerald with his arms in the air and his legs kicked out either side. 'FASTER! FASTER!' he bellowed in her ear. She laughed and then ducked her head forward, urging her broom to zoom even quicker than before, kicking out a flare of green smoke behind them.

'THIS IS AMAZING!' Bill said with a hearty belly laugh. 'But I'm not entirely sure I'm all that keen on HEIGHTS!'

Amethyst cackled as she catapulted them straight up into the air, trailing a stream of purple glitter. They whizzed through the night sky, crossing paths and making beautiful patterns in their wake. Their brooms sped across the moon, and Maggie and Ivy watched as their fathers high-fived each other as they passed.

'Another successful adventure, I'd say!' Maggie reached into her pocket for one of Mrs Anderson's cookies. She split it in half and handed a piece to Ivy.

'Definitely.' Ivy nodded, taking a huge bite and enjoying the explosion of cinnamon in her mouth.

'Shall we have another one next year?' Maggie asked with a grin.

Ivy sighed and rolled her eyes. Knowing her luck, they'd probably never stop having strange magical adventures much like this one. But maybe, just maybe, that wasn't such a bad thing, after all.

Acknowledgements

Crowood Peak wouldn't be the magical place it has become without a town filled with wonderful people helping to create that magic.

Huge love and thanks to my family at Puffin – Carmen McCullough, Philippa Neville, Sarah Connelly, Sarah Doyle, Kat McKenna, Andrea Kearney, Louisa Hunter and Lowri Ribbons! Thank you for believing in the unbelievable. And of course, the incredible Davide Ortu for bringing my characters to life through his sublimely spooky illustrations.

As always, a huge round of applause to my book agent, Hannah Ferguson. Thank you for putting up with all the schedule clashes and theatrical obstacles I throw your way! Huge love also to my team at Curtis Brown who in turn deal with my bookish hurdles with warmth and grace.

Big love as ever to my family! Mum, Dad, Nan, Grandad, Tom, Gi and especially my three gremlin nephews, Buzz, Buddy and Max.

Thanks to my wonderful friends who make my life so magical and keep me going. Scott Paige, Paul Bradshaw, Matt McDonald, Hiba Elchikhe, Matt Gillett, Alex Banks,

Emma Kingston, Rob Houchen, Johnny and Lucy Vickers, Louise Jones, Louise Pentland, Sophie Isaacs, Becky Lock, and if I've forgotten anyone please know you are still very loved!

Thank you to my husband, Joel Montague, for always reminding me you're my number one fan even when I think everything I'm doing is laughably horrendous. Your love and understanding knows no bounds and I know I often try to test that theory, but you never seem to waver. Thank you for choosing me.

Finally, to all the children reading this book. You have so much magic within you! Do whatever you can to keep it alive.

HAVE YOU READ ABOUT
IVY AND MAGGIE'S
FIRST ADVENTURE?

ALSO BY
CARRIE HOPE FLETCHER

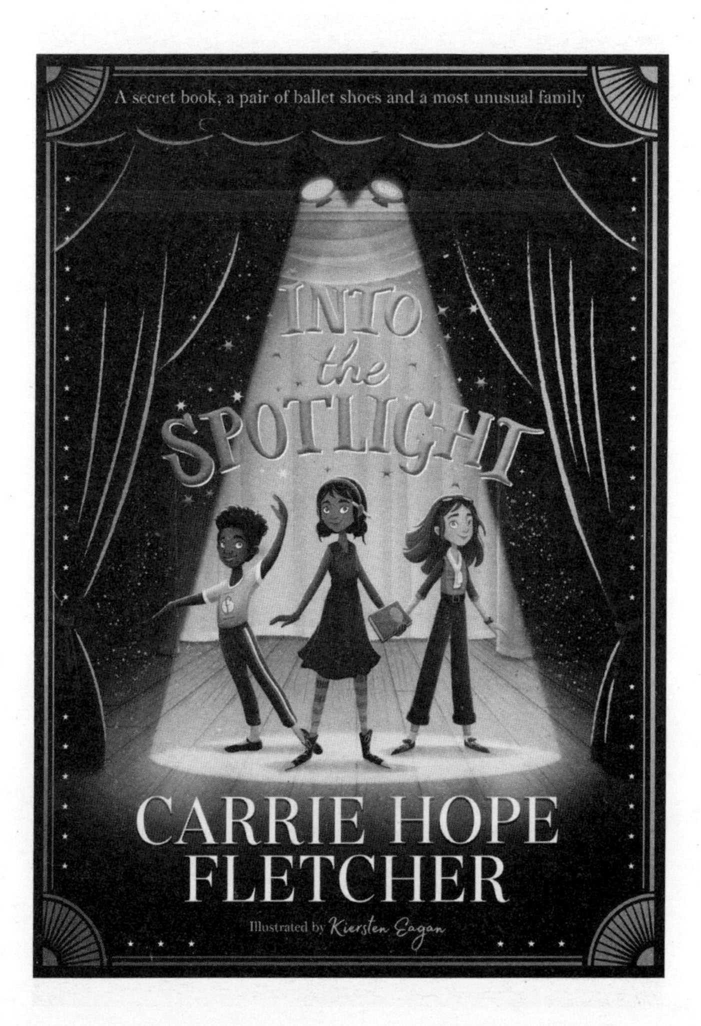